Just One Summer

A Dirty Dares Series Novella

NEW YORK TIMES BESTSELLING AUTHOR

Carly Phillips

JUST ONE SUMMER

One summer. One forbidden temptation. One man who changes everything.

I'm a sheltered twenty-two-year-old virgin with a trust fund—and a future my family already decided for me.

So I run to the Hamptons for the summer to escape.

Then I meet Maddox James.

He's ten years older. Rough-edged. A bar manager who walked away from the money and privilege I was born into. He doesn't trust wealthy women… and he makes sure I know it.

We shouldn't work. But we're thrown together night after night, and the sexual tension between us is impossible to ignore.

I'm completely inexperienced.

Maddox knows precisely what he's doing.

And he's the one man who makes me want to learn.

CHAPTER ONE

Gaby

I SIT IN the library of my parents' summer house, hiding out from all the stuffy guests they invited to their annual dinner party in the Hamptons. These events reek of superiority, something exhibited by my mother, Madeline, my father, Aaron, and everyone else at this event. I'm not like my friends in my social circles. Oh, I learned early on how to play the game well enough, not wanting to stand out or be lonely growing up. But I've never been one of them.

I escaped the party and pulled up the reading app on my phone. I'm in the middle of a steamy romance about a blue-collar guy and a runaway heiress bride who found herself stuck in a small town with a broken-down vehicle.

The author is one of my favorites, her love scenes catnip to a virgin like myself. At twenty-two, I should have given it up long before now, as did most of the girls at the private Manhattan high school I attended. I've been privy to many locker room conversations I wish I could unhear.

The same talks occurred between my *friends* at Columbia University. I graduated a few weeks earlier and wonder if I'll keep any of those friendships, either. The men I met in college weren't any better than the adults in the other room. In other words, full of themselves, entitled, and utterly unappealing.

I'm saving myself for *the one*. If that makes me a romantic, so be it, I think, turning my attention back to my book, where the sexy hero has pinned the heroine against the wall. He's about to take her hard when the creaking sound of the library door opening interrupts my reading.

Annoyed, I look up to find Preston Barrett III standing in the entry. "There you are. Your mother sent me to see where you'd disappeared to."

Of course, she did, since my parents are actively trying to pair me off with Preston in an attempt to cement their status with his family, and to curb my more *common* tendencies. Because for some reason, me enjoying painting and wanting to work instead of giving parties and playing the socialite wife is an embarrassment to them. My parents act like they're the Vanderbilts instead of second-generation wealth.

Preston runs a hand over his perfectly styled blond hair. "You're missing the party."

He picks a nonexistent piece of lint off his light blue Brioni jacket that he matched with navy dress pants and a pale-blue button-down shirt. Navy drivers are on his feet. He is a mini-version of his father, Preston Barrett, Jr. And if I just happen to be name-dropping when taking in his outfit, it's because he does it when bragging, which is often.

I lift one shoulder. "That's the point. It was stuffy with all those people milling around and I was looking for a little privacy." *Why beat around the bush when the truth would do?*

"I *like* the idea of privacy." He closes the door behind him and walks across the room. When he reaches me, he braces his hands on the arms of the chair, his face too close to mine. "You're always playing hard to get with me, Gabriella. How can we get to know one another if you're always pushing me away?"

I breathe in and do my best not to gag or scrunch my nose in disgust. I can't place the type of alcohol on his breath. Mixed with his expensive cologne, it's a tear-inducing smell.

"Come on," he says. "One kiss. You'll see how much you like it."

I haven't kissed him and never will. "I need you to step away from me," I say, my heart pounding in my chest because we're completely alone. I doubt my mother will come looking for me when she'd be only too happy I was making time for Preston.

"Stop playing coy," he says, annoyance in his tone. "You know we're a done deal, right? Your parents want an intimate connection to my family bank. They won't take no for an answer, so let's test our compatibility," he says and smashes his lips against mine.

"Ugh, no." I shove his shoulders, attempting to push him off, but he's stronger and won't budge. Instead he thrusts his tongue in my mouth. I immediately bend my knee and jam it into his groin.

"Dammit!" He steps back, grabbing his nuts and glaring at me. "You didn't have to do that!"

"You didn't hear the word no!" I jump up from my seat and brush past him, rushing for the door while he, hopefully, is taking his time, rubbing his balls before returning to the party.

I run down the hall, bypassing the living area full of guests. Then, not wanting to call attention to myself, I slow as I approach the front door.

"Gabriella?"

Only one person could stop me from fleeing. I turn toward my widowed grandmother Annabelle, who is my father's mother. Due to her debilitating arthritis, she lives with us and has her own wing in each of the family homes, where she stays with her full-time caregiver. My grandmother has been my main source of affection growing up and understands me in uncanny ways.

"Grandma, I need to get out of here."

Annabelle narrows her green-eyed gaze. "I saw that weasel Preston, stumbling out of the library holding his balls. Did he try something?" she asks, raising her cane and waving it in the air. For her age, Annabelle is as insightful as a woman raised in modern times.

A much-needed smile comes to my lips. "Thanks, but I handled him."

"Aah. That was from you," my grandmother says with a wry grin. "I don't know what your parents are thinking, expecting you to marry that spoiled, obnoxious excuse for a man." She shakes her head. "Aaron is my son but money changed him. Your mother, too," she says, making a dismayed clucking sound. "I lost the argument when it came to your sister, but she never had your spirit and was willing to do their bidding. You need to fly, my beautiful girl."

A lump rises in my throat because without my grandmother, I would be the oddball, lost in my staid family. "I love you, Grandma." I pull the frail woman into a hug.

"I love you too. Now go before they come looking. I'll cover." With a wave, my grandmother turns back toward the party.

When I get older I want to be a badass like Annabelle, I think, as I let myself outside and ask a valet to bring my car, a gift from Annabelle for my college graduation.

Once settled inside the vehicle, I take off. Away from the house and feeling free, I know just where I want to go. The Back Door is a bar I visited last summer when they first opened their Hamptons location. The atmosphere is casual, fun and best of all, nobody will come looking for me there.

Maddox

I WALK INTO The Back Door, the bar I manage, and nod at the hostess waiting to serve the guests who prefer tables to standing around the bar.

"Everything quiet?" I ask Sheila, who has been with the place since our opening. I came on a few months after.

"Yes. Nice turnover in the dining area."

A glance tells me every table is full, with more people waiting outside. The owners, Zach Dare and Remy Sterling, will be pleased.

I nod. "Keep up the good work," I say, then walk straight through to the bar where Cal, the head bartender, holds down the fort. "What's going on tonight?" I ask.

Cal looks up from the glass he's holding and wiping down the counter with a rag. "The usual," he says. "And I've been keeping an eye on her." He tilts his head toward the end of the bar.

Following his gaze, I see a pretty, young blonde stirring her frozen drink with a straw. She wears a halter-top that covers her neck and ends with a soft ruffle beneath her chin. Her arms are tanned, her skin golden, and her soft hair falls over her shoulders, straight and silky.

She mixes the drink, staring into the glass, something obviously weighing heavily on her mind. From her dainty movements to her clearly expensive clothes, and gold Cartier Love bracelet gleaming on her delicate wrist, every instinct I've honed over the years and learned from my brief but lucrative career on Wall Street, tells me she comes from wealth.

So why is she drinking here where the common people gather and not at Daddy's social club?

As I watch, her pink lips purse around the straw, and my cock twitches in my pants.

Fuck. Seems I learned my lesson about spoiled rich girls but my dick hasn't gotten the message. "Did you card her?" I ask Cal.

"Of course, boss. She's legal."

"Barely, I'm sure," I mutter.

"Excuse me, Cal!" the woman under discussion calls out, waving a hand to get his attention.

"On a first name basis already?" I ask.

The bartender turns her way. "What can I get you, princess?"

"Princess?"

Cal shrugs. "What can I say? She's a drunk-talker, and I gave her a nickname."

She points to her glass, indicating she'd like another.

"How many margaritas has she had?"

Cal shrugs. "This would be her fourth. But I was going to cut her off. She's been going at it since she walked in a little over an hour ago. Rich girl with rich girl problems. I kinda feel sorry for her."

"Excuse me," another patron calls out, an annoyed tone in his voice. "Can someone get me a refill?"

"Coming," Cal says.

"And I'll take care of the princess." I sigh and stride over to her end of the bar.

She glances up with glassy eyes that grow wide at the sight of me. "Well, hi there." Her gaze rakes over me, approval obvious from her small smile.

"Hi yourself, princess."

She perks up at the nickname. "Why can't my parents want me to marry someone who looks like you?" Glassy emerald-green eyes fringed by long, black lashes, stare up at me longingly.

I shake my head and ignore her comment.

"Can I get another one please?" She points

to her margarita glass, purses her lips around the straw and sips, making a loud slurping sound. "See? It's empty!" The noise is unattractive, but her subsequent giggle isn't.

I groan. "I think you've had enough."

She lifts one delicate shoulder. "I'll ask Cal. He liked me." She looks beyond me. "Oh, Cal! Woo-hoo!" She waves a hand in the air to get the other man's attention.

I turn and shake my head at the bartender.

"Sorry," Cal says loudly.

She sighs. "You're mean."

"And you're drunk." I pick up her glass, turn and put it in the rack before facing her again.

She sits with both elbows on the bar, a forlorn look on her face.

I sigh. "Okay, what's the problem?" I ask, knowing if I'm behind the bar, I have no choice but to play psychiatrist without a diploma.

First, I pour her a soda from the tap, then I walk over and place it in front of her with a new straw, prepared to listen.

"My parents are pressuring me to get together with a guy of *their* choosing." She makes a disgusted face, letting me know what she thinks of the man.

I shake my head. Typical rich parents with 18th-century expectations. Marry off their beautiful daughter to someone equally wealthy and acceptable in their eyes. I saw it so often during my years on Wall Street, watched it up close at dinner parties I was invited to. Though I was new to their world, I also came up quickly, made a name for myself and was considered a prime catch.

I almost feel sorry for the princess, but I have no doubt with the *right* man, she'd be all in to do what her parents ask of her. All the women in her social circle do. And though I wanted the money, having grown up solidly lower middle class, it wasn't my scene. Something I learned pretty quickly.

"They had a party tonight with the typical Hamptons crowd," she says, bringing me out of my thoughts. "I escaped to the library to get away from everyone and he found me." She wipes her lips with the back of her hand, and I stiffen.

"Did he touch you?"

She nods. "He planted a big slobbery kiss on me. But I kicked him in the balls and ran out."

I'm unable to stifle a laugh at her actions,

but the thought of any man putting a hand on her soft skin has my temper rising. Though she's definitely too young for me, I can't deny the initial attraction. One I'll ignore.

She lets out a loud sigh. "*Now* can I have another drink?"

I shake my head. "Sorry. You're officially cut off for the night."

"Boss, you're needed in the kitchen," one of the bar backs calls out.

I glance at the young woman who is checking her phone. "I'll be right back."

I walk to the kitchen and through the swinging door where I find myself in the middle of an argument between a busboy and waitress who've been dating. Doing my best not to lose my temper, I remind them that if they can't get along, one of them will have to go. The duo, I'm not certain if they are still a couple, rush back to work.

Another fifteen to twenty minutes pass, during which I put out a few more fires, reminding me of why I prefer to have things run without me in the kitchen. Problems are typically solved by the staff if they don't have the manager to run interference.

By the time I make my way back to the bar,

the crowd has grown, the crowd is hopping and Cal has been joined by Eddie, the newest summer hire. While Cal is professionally moving between the patrons, removing full drinks and serving fresh ones, Eddie lingers at the far end of the bar.

It's obvious why. The pretty princess has an empty glass in front of her, and I watch as the bartender swaps it for a fresh margarita. Then, instead of moving to the next person waiting, he leans closer and begins to chat, while she flutters her lashes and stirs the new drink she shouldn't have been served.

I stride over and swoop up the glass before she can put those slick, freshly glossed lips around the straw.

"Eddie, get back to work!" I bark, tilting my head toward a point away from the customers. "We'll talk soon."

"Yeah, boss." The man slinks away, and I turn to join him for a reprimand.

"Oh, come on, party pooper. Eddie had no issue serving me," *my* princess complains.

I ignore my automatic use of the pronoun. She's already on a first name basis with both my bartenders and is now slurring her words, something that wouldn't have happened if

Eddie did his job instead of flirting with her.

I turn back to find her wrinkling her nose in a pout I find too cute. I need to get control of this situation, starting with something I should have done earlier, but I trusted Cal. Still do, but I need to see for myself.

"Are you sure you're twenty-one?" I ask.

She hiccups. "Twenty-two." She holds up two fingers. "See?"

"How about a license and not the peace sign?"

She rolls her eyes and leans down, probably to find her handbag, nearly toppling to the floor. The guy nearest her steps aside instead of helping.

"Jackass," I mutter. "Are you okay?"

"Fine." She slides off the chair and kneels this time, her head disappearing beneath the bar before she pops up, purse in hand. "Got it!" She fishes inside, retrieves a small, zippered pouch with a familiar logo on the side, and finally hands me her license.

I study it with interest. "Gabriella Annabelle Davenport." I say the mouthful out loud.

"My friends call me Gabby," she says, now leaning both arms on the counter, looking like she needs to be held up.

Something I really wouldn't mind doing, which tells me I need my head examined, both because I recognize her last name—assuming she is Aaron Davenport of Davenport Securities' daughter—and at…yes, twenty-two, I am ten years her senior.

"Okay, Gabby—"

She bursts out laughing, interrupting me. "I lied! Nobody calls me Gabby except my sister. And now you. You're my friend, right?"

"Not if that means you think I'm giving you another drink," I say.

She sticks her little tongue out in response and dammit, my mind goes into overdrive, imagining all the things she could do with that soft tongue, like lick the length of my stiff dick.

"How about you give me your address, and I'll call an Uber to take you home?"

She shakes her head, her blonde waves creating a halo around her head before settling back on her bare shoulders. "No. I do not want to go back there." Her eyes are glassy but determined.

Recalling what she told me happened to her earlier tonight, I can't be a bastard and insist she go home. Besides, her license, which I put on the counter in front of her, has a New York

City address, and I have no idea where her parents' summer home is located.

"Okay, is there someone else you can call for a ride? Or a friend whose house you can go to?"

She replaces her license in the small zipper purse and shoves it back into her bag. "I don't have any friends I trust enough to help me," she says quietly.

An odd statement, I think. "Somehow I doubt someone as chatty as you are doesn't have girlfriends." I cock an eyebrow.

"I'm different," she says, not meeting my gaze, and something in my chest twists at the honest admission.

"How about we sober you up and discuss it more after?"

"Boss?" This time it's Sheila who calls for me, coming up beside Gabby. "I need you. There's an obnoxious patron giving Lizzie a hard time," she says of one of our newer waitresses.

I nod. "Coming." I look at Gabby. "I'll have Cal get you some coffee and water. Later, I'll make sure you get home safe." As the acting bar manager, it's my responsibility.

And that's true, but my gut tells me my need

to look out for her goes deeper. Something that makes no sense. Not for a woman I just met and is too young for me.

I give her one last glance, and her gaze locks with mine, definite interest in her expression. Double shit. I don't need the unwanted feeling reciprocated.

"I need to go deal with that problem," I tell her in a gruff voice. "But I'll be back."

I'm about to turn when she speaks. "Wait."

"What is it?"

She rubs one finger over her pouty bottom lip in a gesture I don't think she means as seductive. But it is.

"I don't know your name," she says.

"It's Maddox." I turn to go deal with the problem up front.

"Sexy name for a sexy guy," Gabby murmurs.

I hear the words as I take my first step away and my ego preens at the compliment. My unruly cock likes it, too. She's more trouble than I originally thought.

Trouble in a sweet yet sultry, innocent yet vixenish package. One I'll have a problem resisting if I don't get her home and away from me. Soon. I've already had one experience with a rich woman slumming with a bar manager. While I was thinking about the future, she was using me until summer ended. Lesson learned. Unfortunately, I've been celibate ever since, which makes my attraction to Gabby harder to ignore.

But I will.

A couple of hours later, the bar is still busy. Cal offers to close for me, a job the other man often handles.

I've been keeping an eye on, and my distance from, Gabby as she drinks coffee and stares into the cup as if she'll find life's answers inside.

Unable to ignore her any longer, I come up behind her and tap her bare shoulder, finding her skin soft and welcoming under my calloused fingertips.

She turns in her seat. "Maddox!" she exclaims like she hasn't seen me in days.

"Okay, princess. Time's up. Where do you live?" With any luck, her parents' party is over by now, and she can go home.

"My car is in the back parking lot, but don't worry, I know I can't drive."

One battle I don't have to fight. "Okay, so let's call you an Uber. What's your address?"

She bats those long lashes and treats me to a sweet smile and a lazy shrug. "I don't remember," she says, giving away her lie with an adorable smirk. She slides off the stool and attempts to stand but is wobbly on her heels and they aren't all that high.

Still drunk.

Jesus. I step forward and slide an arm around her waist, intending to steady her. The move has her falling against me. I try to grab her and accidentally brush the side of her full breast with my hand.

I pray she doesn't notice, but she stills at my touch and instead of pulling away, she leans further into me.

Her strawberry scent reaches my nostrils, and I breathe in deep, my body too aware of her body heat against me. All night I've been trying not to react to the strange pull I feel toward her, and now she's in my arms.

"What am I going to do with you?" I ask in a rough whisper.

I can't leave her here. Can't force her to give up her address. Nor do I want to take her somewhere she doesn't feel safe, even if that is her home.

The answer nudges at me, and I try to think

of any solution other than taking her to my half-finished house and letting her stay over. But damned if I can come up with an alternative.

With a groan, I shift her so she once again stands on her own two feet. "Okay, princess. Let's go."

She looks up at me with trusting eyes. Too trusting, considering the desire that rides me and insists I put her to sleep *in my bed*. Beside me. And when she wakes up tomorrow, sober, I can settle myself on top of her and slide my now hard-as-nails cock into her soft, wet, willing body.

Which will not be happening.

"Where are we going?" she asks.

"My place. I have a guestroom," I mutter and help her weave around the crowd.

As I pass the hostess stand, Sheila shoots me a questioning look. Not once since I took this job have I left with a customer. I don't want to think about how bad it looks as I walk out with my arm around Gabby.

When we reach my Wrangler, I help her into the passenger seat, grab the seatbelt and reach over to buckle her in.

"You're such a gentleman," she says, her slur heavier now that she can relax and let the alcohol inside her system take over.

I shake my head. "And you're lucky I am. Imagine if someone other than me found you tonight." My hands curl into fists at the thought. I shut her door and come around the driver's side.

I drive to my house, a fixer-upper on the beach I invested a huge chunk of savings in to buy and renovate myself. After my years working on Wall Street, trying to be someone I'm not in order to make money to help my parents and younger brother, I found myself miserable despite the wealth. I retreated from that life and returned to my roots, working with my hands, managing a bar, and feeling better about the man I want to be.

Apparently, that man has a savior complex when it comes to one particular drunk, rich, pretty *young* woman. Who knew?

By the time I reach my place, a short ten-minute drive, she's fallen asleep against the door. I park in my driveway and turn off the ignition, climbing out and walking around to the passenger side.

I open the door, making sure to catch her before she leans too far outside the car, unbuckle her seatbelt, and lift her into my arms. Her breasts press against my chest, allowing me to feel her curves and imagine those breasts bare, her nipples dusky pink and rigid with need.

Sucking in a sharp breath, I ignore my uncomfortable hard-on and walk the three steps up to the front door. Her eyes open at the bouncing motion. Emerald-green orbs stare up at me, but instead of wariness, I see more trust, backed up when she doesn't try to wiggle out of my grasp and stand on her own.

Instead, she lets out a contented sigh, wraps her arms around my neck and lays her head against my chest. Desire ramps up inside me, thoughts of peeling off her oh-so appropriate silk top and suckling on her tight nipples rushing through my head.

Fuck.

I'm going to hell for the things I want to do with the woman in my arms. Even knowing our age difference, I can't convince myself it matters. Not in my daydreams, anyway. Reality is a whole different ballgame. I am a master at self-control.

Even so, I have no doubt I'll jerk off to that vision in the shower, then toss and turn, the scent of strawberries forever embedded in my brain.

CHAPTER TWO

Gabby

I WAKE UP to the sun streaming through a window and searing into my eyes. I immediately close them tight. And as last night comes back to me in a technicolor movie-like reel, I groan. I might have been drunk last night, and I'm definitely hungover this morning, but I remember every detail.

I was mauled by Preston at my parents' party, rushed from the house, and ended up at The Back Door where a nice bartender named Cal served me drinks, and then *he* showed up. The man who brought me to his house because I refused to give him my parents' address. After consoling myself with the fact that at least I didn't throw up in his car, I force my eyelids open and blink into the sun.

I take stock. The headache is to be expected. No nausea, thank God. And I'm still in my dress from last night while my shoes are on the floor by the bed. The hot bartender, Maddox, I remember, didn't take advantage of me. He brought me home and took care of me, making him a decent guy.

There's an old-fashioned shade on the window which hasn't been rolled down, explaining my bright wakeup call. I look around and see bare walls with holes where picture hooks once were, faded rectangles where pictures once hung.

On the nightstand, I'm surprised to find a tall glass of water and two Ibuprofen. I'm touched by the thoughtful gesture from a stranger whose hospitality I'm already taking advantage of, and very grateful. I sit up, immediately swallowing the pills and downing the entire glass of water. With a little luck, between this and some food, I'll get rid of the pounding headache. Once I have a clear head, I can figure out what to do next.

I swing my legs over the side of the bed and look around, noticing my purse on the wooden dresser across from me. My phone is inside it, and I'm not ready to see the dozens of messages my mother probably left. Still, I'm not a procrastinator and decide it's better to know what awaits me. I retrieve my cell and turn it on, wincing at the text messages, missed calls, and voicemails.

A quick scroll through reveals my mother is furious that I *embarrassed the family by leaving*, my grandmother urges me to check in, and Preston informs me I've had my fun and it's time to *come home and face up to my responsibilities. Asshole.*

I leave my phone on the dresser with my purse and walk into the hall, finding a bathroom across from the room where I slept. Once I'm inside and lock the door, I see he left me a toothbrush, toothpaste, and towels on the counter, along with what looks like one of his t-shirts.

I blow out a long breath, wondering how I got so lucky to find a good guy in my drunken state. The bathroom is basic. The toilet is a standard, and the sink white porcelain with a small two-door wood vanity. I turn on the shower water, adjust the temperature, undress and step under the warm spray. There's soap along with generic bottles of shampoo and conditioner, and I gratefully use them all. A little while later, I step out of the bathroom feeling clean and refreshed and wearing a soft tee-shirt that falls to my knees, and yesterday's underwear I turned inside out. I stop in my room to take a hair tie out of my bag and pull my long hair into a messy bun on top of my head.

I glance in the mirror. My cheeks are pink from drinking and my eyes a little glassy, but without access to makeup, there isn't much more I can do. Last night, I made a fool of myself, and I have to face the bartender and see whether he's as good-looking as I remember. Or if I was viewing him through a drunken lens.

The house doesn't appear to be big, and it's definitely under renovation. As I make my way to the kitchen, I notice the walls in the large family room have been primed but only one is painted, and there's furniture, a mahogany-colored leather sofa and matching club chair and a large steamer-trunk as a cocktail table. No knickknacks, nothing giving the place a homey feel. I walk toward what I assume is the kitchen, glancing out the sliding glass doors as I pass. The patio is also being worked on, the dirt outside having been dug up and most of the old bluestone removed except for a few square stones providing a walking path to the sandy area behind it.

I stop in the kitchen entry, taking in the obviously new, stainless-steel appliances, a swirled mix of gray, white, and black granite countertops, and a weathered wood tile on the floor in a steel gray. It's masculine and very much like the man I remember meeting last night.

Speaking of my host, he stands in front of the sink, looking out a window. With no shirt, a pair of black track pants ride low on his hips. Defined muscles are visible in his upper back, tapering down to a lean waist. From behind, he's an extremely hot man, and I swallow hard, and wrong, and begin to cough and choke on my own saliva.

He turns at the sound, his gaze landing on me. I blink, and tears drip down my face as I struggle to catch my breath while taking in the hotness before me. No drunken goggles for me. The man is the perfect male specimen, his dark hair tousled from sleep, his brown eyes warm, and his tanned body a picture of muscled goodness with a tattoo on one shoulder.

His eyes soften in concern. "You okay?"

I nod and swipe at the wetness on my cheeks. "Swallowed wrong."

Once I stop coughing, his gaze drifts from my face, traveling down my body. I might not have a ton of experience, but his eyes definitely heat, and I glance down to find my nipples poking through my thin cotton tee. *His* T-shirt.

Embarrassed, I fold my arms across my chest, and he immediately turns away.

He takes a few steps to the fridge, pulls out a carton, grabs a glass from a cabinet and pours orange juice into the cup. "Here."

Grateful, I accept the drink and take a long sip, keeping my body angled away from him. I drink, waiting to be sure I won't choke again before answering. "Thank you. And thanks for…bringing me back here, leaving me water and something for my head. Just…everything."

"Wasn't like you gave me a choice," he says in a wry tone, and my cheeks heat with more embarrassment.

I hadn't given him my parents' address, but I can't say I'm sorry. "Well, I appreciate it."

He studies me intently, as if trying to figure me out. I'm aware of him now firmly keeping his eyes on my face, and I relax. If he finds me attractive, I definitely return the sentiment but I'd rather have more coverage while talking to him.

"Hungry?" he asks. "I have bagels." He gestures to the counter where a bag of varied flavors sits. "Butter and cream cheese are in the fridge."

I nod. "Thank you."

I walk past him and set about choosing my bagel, a cinnamon raisin, and taking a tub of cream cheese from the refrigerator. "Want one?"

"I already ate."

I shrug. Making myself at home isn't easy, but I do my best, toasting and making my bagel, pouring a cup of coffee from the pot that he already made, and sitting down at the small kitchen table with him leaning against the counter, watching me the entire time. He is respectful, keeping his gaze off my chest, but I notice him taking in my tanned legs, and I think I hear a hum of approval before he clears his throat and glances out the window.

"So your house is being renovated?" I ask as I take a bite of my bagel.

He cocks an eyebrow at my interest. "Yeah."

"I like it here. It's cozy. I mean, except for the lack of pictures and…feminine touches." Yes, I'm hinting for an answer as to whether he has a girlfriend.

He frowns in confusion. "Why the hell would I have feminine touches?"

I shrug. "Your girlfriend likes the sparse décor?" Yes, I'm curious and digging for information. He might be a touch grumpy, but I can't deny the hotness factor. Nobody in my world looks like him.

"I don't have a girlfriend."

I grin. "Interesting." And good to know.

He exhales an exasperated breath and runs a hand through his sexy, somewhat long hair. "Look, can you just finish up so I can take you to the bar to get your car and you can go home?"

I'm obviously irritating him, but for some reason, I like getting under his skin. He might not want me here but from the way he looks at me, he's not immune.

"I'm not going home. Not while my parents are giving the asshole access to the house and by default, to me."

His sigh tells me he understands, but his next words are, "Well you can't stay here," he says gruffly.

I slowly put the bagel onto the plate, considering my options. All the hotels, motels, and rentals will be booked for the summer. My friends' parents won't take me in out of loyalty to my mother and father, who will never believe me if I tell them what Preston did. People in our circle close ranks. I know I'll find myself on the outside, with our friends helping my parents to push me to return home.

I truly have no other options, which means I'll have to play on his sympathy and hope his kindness and hospitality continue. Okay, kindness might be stretching how he's treated me, but he brought me here, gave me a room, clean clothing and breakfast. He might be grumpy, but he hasn't turned me away. Until now.

"Look, I realize we don't know each other but you do have an extra room. The one I slept in last night." I've never been so pushy, but I really need more time to figure out my life.

He shakes his head. "It's about to become a study."

"But for now, there's still a bed." I bat my eyelashes in a futile attempt to flirt, but I've never been any good at it.

He studies me, those chocolate brown eyes taking me in. He's good at hiding his emotions. I'll just have to be better at breaking through his walls.

Maddox

I STARE AT my too-innocent looking guest and groan. She gives off a guileless appearance, but Gabby knows just how to work me to get what she wants. I doubt she's evil or manipulative like many women I've been unlucky enough to meet. Just young and desperate, which has her chipping holes in my defenses. Not that I'll show her as much.

She's adorably cute and extremely sexy in my overly long T-shirt. I'm not used to women wearing my clothing and seeing her in my thin tee does something for me. Her legs are lean, tanned, and I can imagine them wrapped around my waist as I back her into a wall, kiss her hard and slide my hand beneath the hem of that shirt, stroking her wet sex to make her come. *Those* are the reasons I'm fighting so hard against her staying. I cannot allow myself to get involved with her. She's too young, which might mean too flighty.

But there's something about the innocence I sense that calls to me. No other woman I've been with, especially not Felicia, who I dated for six months and thought I was falling for, had this appealing, wholesome side to her.

Felicia was elegant and looked perfect on my arm at any event we attended, but she lacked the genuine warmth Gabby possesses. And at the very mention of me possibly resigning my job at the investment firm, she lost her mind, yelling, shouting, and threatening to break up with me, and that was before I revealed my intention to leave the rat race and move here.

No sooner did she react than I knew I had to end things. Learning she wasn't in love with me but with my status was a blow, but at least I walked away with my dignity intact. Only with hindsight did I realize I liked similar things about her, how we fit together for business and yes, the sex was good. As shallow as I discovered the relationship was, the road to getting over her still wasn't easy.

My temporary houseguest already evokes protective emotions and those feelings make me weak. If she stays, I might give in, and I refuse to fall for the poor little rich girl. One who could decide to run back to her rich family and leave me alone to pick up the pieces. Been there, done that. I don't care for a repeat.

"Maddox?" Gabby waves a hand in front of my face. "Are you listening?"

I groan, aware I've been lost in thought for

way too long. "Look, you don't have to go home but you can't stay here." It was hard enough to sleep knowing she was a short distance away in my study, on the bed my brother used while he lived here. My shower consisted of jerking off to thoughts of Gabby and being too pissed off at myself to fall asleep after. "How about we get dressed, drive over to the bar, and you can figure something out?"

She shakes her head. "I already thought things through. Everything around here is booked in the summer, rentals included. I'm not going back to the city. My parents will follow. And I am not going to their summer home so my mother can push her agenda, forcing me to hang around with that rich, handsy loser, *Preston Barrett, III,* thinking I'll agree to marry him."

"You said Preston Barrett?" I know that name.

"The third." She wrinkles her nose in distaste.

I agree with her assessment of the prick her parents want her to marry. I know him too well.

"You know him?" she asks, her eyes wide in surprise.

I can't prevent the half smile from lifting my lips. I didn't plan on revealing anything personal, but with this common connection, I can't hold back. "If I told you before I managed The Back Door, I was a money manager in the city, would you believe me?"

"Why wouldn't I?" she asks without hesitation. "It just makes me want to know what made you move here and change your whole life."

I blink, surprised at her nonjudgmental reaction. Even my parents, who love me with everything in them, wondered if I lost my mind when I made the choice. In the end, they supported me and are grateful that I'm happy again.

I don't reply to her question. "So I know the Barretts because I worked at Barrett Senior's financial firm."

"Aah. So you know the slime is inherited?" She grins, and I want nothing more than to kiss those lips.

I nod. "Preston came in thinking he was above the existing partners because of his family name. He cornered more than one receptionist, sending them running to HR only to find nobody would write up the owner's son." It's just one of the many reasons that world isn't for me.

"That's awful," Gabby whispers, obviously putting herself in the place of those women.

"You defended yourself against him. As for me, I saw him in action, then backed up my assistant's accusation. I put it in writing, but I assume Senior buried the claims. She left the firm when I did. You're doing the right thing, getting away from him."

And shame on her parents for thinking the entitled young bastard with the wandering hands is good enough for their daughter. And there are those possessive instincts firing up again. Ones I never felt for a female in my life, except for my mother.

"Thank you for saying that." Gabby smiles. "So you see why I'm not going home to deal with my family or Preston." She squares her shoulders, obviously preparing for an argument.

Oh, she's good. Using my disgust with Barrett as a way to change my mind about her staying. I grind my teeth so hard I'm surprised I don't chip a molar. Because there is no way I can send her back to the pit of vipers she came from.

"Fine. You can stay here." I'll just have to take an extra cold shower a day.

Her eyes open wide, a big smile pulling at

her mouth. "Really?"

I hold up a hand. "For a little while. Just until you figure out your next move."

"Thank you!" Ignoring the last bite of her breakfast, she jumps up from her seat. Next thing I know, she's wrapped herself around me, hugging me tight. "I'm so grateful. You've been a lifesaver from the moment we met."

I find myself surrounded by her warm body, soft curves and the fragrance of the generic shampoo and soap in the shower. Her bland scent does nothing to calm my desire or arousal because I've already inhaled her strawberry scent when I carried her to bed last night. The sweet smell lingers in my memory and my body reacts to everything about her, my cock growing harder.

She doesn't let go, and I reach up, gripping her wrists with every intention of unwinding her limbs from around my neck. Anything to create distance between us before I do something I'll regret.

Taking my cue, her arms drift to her sides, but she doesn't step back. Oh, no. Not the woman who has trouble written all over her. Instead, she tilts her head and meets my gaze. Her emerald eyes glitter like precious jewels, a combination of desire and naughtiness in her expression. "You try really hard to hide it but you're a nice guy, Maddox. Thank you."

My name on her lips is my undoing. I take in her half-lidded gaze and natural, pink puckered mouth and when she rises on to her tiptoes, I shove all rational thought aside and dip my head to steal a taste. She is all in, her kiss eager but inexperienced, solidifying the innocence I sensed from the minute I laid eyes on her. Instead of being a turn-off, it only makes me want her more.

I slide my tongue further into her mouth, and she meets me with a greedy passion I didn't think her capable of. And fuck, she tastes good, like strawberry cream cheese and coffee, and everything sweet. I'm not used to sweet and want more. Gripping the back of her neck, I hold her in place, devouring her mouth.

Her little moans are hot and when she begins to press her body into mine, I'm shocked I don't come in my pants. I never had such an explosive first kiss. On that thought, reality comes back with a jarring thud.

I lift my head and take a step back, needing the distance. I end things before I say screw it, lay her out on the kitchen table and make a feast of her sweet body. She blinks up at me, her dark lashes fluttering over her eyes, and I hold onto her forearms, making certain she's steady on her feet.

"This was a bad idea," I say, releasing her.

"What was?" Her tongue swipes over her damp lower lip, and I stifle a groan.

"Us. This. You and me." I gesture back and forth between us. "If you're going to stay here, it's hands off."

"Lips, too?" she asks.

There's no need for a reply, so I pin her with my gaze until she looks away, then folds her arms across her chest in a protective measure. She still pulls in deep inhales, attempting to catch her breath from our kiss. And the flush in her cheeks could have been from arousal but I have a feeling she's also embarrassed I pushed her away.

Dammit. I feel bad, but even if she wasn't going to be my houseguest, we can't get involved.

"Why does it have to be hands off?" she asks, surprising me.

She's pushy. Brave. And I admire those qualities. "For many reasons, not the least of which is I'm ten years older than you."

For another, she could grow bored with me and my minimalistic lifestyle compared to the wealth she grew up with. And though she might not want Preston the douche, I have no doubt she wants marriage, kids, and everything I decided against after my relationship with Felicia went up in flames. Gabby doesn't need someone who has a decade of life experience on her, and who walked away from the wealth she grew up with and no doubt will go back to. Eventually.

She purses her lips and stops arguing or asking questions.

Both things put me on edge. One thing I already learned, she doesn't give up easily. "So we're on the same page? This…we…aren't happening?" I need her to agree.

"Fine." Her lips purse but she remains silent.

I narrow my gaze, waiting for another argument. When I don't get one, I let out a relieved breath. "Good. Get ready. We'll go to the bar and you can drive your car back here."

She treats me to a salute.

Smart ass, I think, unable to hold back a grin.

She pauses by the table and begins to clean

up her breakfast, putting the food back in the fridge, and washing her dish and coffee mug in the sink. I have no doubt she's grown up with help, so this display impresses me. Felicia always left hers in the sink for me to clean.

Without a word, Gabby strides out of the kitchen, leaving me to watch her hips sway as she makes her exit and causing me to wonder how that ass would fit in my palms.

"Not happening," I remind myself and storm out of the room, heading to my bedroom to change.

★　★　★

Gabby

WE ARE SO happening, I think. No matter what Maddox says. That kiss was the most incredible thing I ever felt. If he thinks his silly words will deter me, he doesn't know me very well. Which he doesn't. Something I hope to correct during my stay with him.

And though I might be a little innocent...okay, *very* innocent, I know he was as into it as I was. My panties are soaked, and I felt the hard ridge of his erection pulsing against my lower body, evidence of his desire. I didn't ask to stay because I'm fascinated by the sexy bartender, but I won't lie and say it isn't an added bonus to avoiding my family until I make some life decisions.

Once back in the bedroom, I put on my dress from last night, doing my best to smooth out the wrinkles and knowing I fail. Looks like I'll be experiencing the walk of shame without the benefit of any orgasms the night before. Based on how my body responded to Maddox, I wonder how easily he could be persuaded to change his mind about us.

Not that I plan to give him my virginity, but there are other things we could do, and I'm pretty certain a man who looks like him is talented. I want to be one of the recipients of what he can surely offer me. His hard muscles tempt me, and I want to run my hands over his tanned skin and lick every available inch of his tattoo.

My phone rings, causing me to jump at the unexpected sound. I glance at the screen. I squeal, grateful for the distraction from thinking of Maddox naked and take the call. "Hi, P!"

"Hi, yourself," my sister Penelope says. "Grandma tells me you had quite the night. Can

I ask where you are?" The concern in her tone is obvious and I sigh.

"I think it's better if I don't tell you. Plausible deniability, you know?"

"Then tell me you're safe."

"Very," I assure her. Penelope is the only other person who I know supports me. "I'm staying with a…friend."

"You don't have any real friends in the Hamptons, Gabby. Who are you with?"

I bite down on the inside of my cheek. "A good man. I swear. You need to trust me. I know what I'm doing. I refuse to marry or even date that asshole who won't take no for an answer."

"What?" my sister yells. "Did he—"

"No! I kneed him in the balls and left the house but nobody cares. Nobody but Grandma, anyway. It's time I take a stand, P. I have goals and things I want out of life. Not only don't our parents approve, they actively blackballed me."

Penelope sighs. "I know, and I'm sorry. Their reach is far. But you have your painting, and you are so talented. Your canvases are natural and evoke so many emotions. Why not try to sell your work? I have everything you've done stored in the basement. Nobody can take that away from you."

Closing my eyes, I agree. "Yeah." I need to believe in myself to take that step.

"Five minutes, and I'm leaving," Maddox calls out, his voice deep through my closed bedroom door.

"I have to go, but I'll be in touch," I tell my sister.

"Okay. I'm proud of you, holding out for true love and the life *you* want," Penelope says, and in her words, I hear my older sister's regrets for marrying a man our parents chose. "I never had your passion or courage. I'm happy, I have my baby, and Stu is a good man. The guy they chose for you isn't. Stand firm, Gabby. Love you."

I swallow over the lump in my throat. "Love you, too. Can I ask one favor?"

"Anything. You know that."

"Call Grandma. Tell her you heard from me, and I'm safe, and I'll get in touch when I'm ready. I'm sure Mom or Dad is monitoring her and her phone."

Penelope sighs. "I will if you promise to keep in touch so I know you're safe with your new *friend.*"

"Promise. Talk soon." I disconnect the call.

After gathering my purse and taking a quick look in the mirror, I walk out to meet Maddox.

I find him standing by the front door, jingling his keys in one hand.

"Ready!"

His gaze locks on mine, and he frowns as he takes in my outfit.

"Yes, I'm in yesterday's clothes," I say, reading his mind. "I can't go out in your shirt, so I don't have much of a choice. But once I stop at an ATM, I can fix that. I need to pull out some cash before my father either cuts me off or empties the account."

Though I have a trust fund given to me by my grandparents, I can't access the money until I turn thirty. I can withdraw the interest that's deposited, but I can't access the account in the Hamptons. My checking account was funded by my parents during college, and until I get a job, I'm stuck relying on them. My grandmother would give me money, but I hate to ask, wanting to figure out a way to stand on my own two feet.

"If I remember correctly, there's an ATM near the bar, right?" I ask.

"There is. Come on." He opens the door and tips his head, indicating I should walk through.

Passing him, I inhale and am treated to his masculine scent, one I recognize as sandalwood. A warm, exotic fragrance with hints of vanilla, it's my favorite smell. My interest in the arts and sciences are varied, and I've taken courses in fragrance making at the Fashion Institute of Technology, using trust fund money my parents can't track. No way do I want to hear them complain about wasting time and money. I eventually settled into art history, but my memory of different scents remains clear.

And Maddox's scent, especially when we're enclosed in his Jeep, makes me want to crawl into his lap, bury my face in his neck and breathe him in for as long as he lets me.

He remains quiet on the trip into town, and I respect his obvious need for silence. I invaded his life enough already.

He parks behind the bar near my convertible, and we both get out of the Jeep. "I take it that's yours?" He gestures to the BMW.

I nod. "But I'll be in town for a while. I want to do some shopping after the bank."

He works the house key off the holder and hands it to me. "There's a hardware store on the corner of Main. Make yourself a copy and bring me the original when you're through."

Surprised, I curl my fingers around the key in his hand, sliding over the roughened calluses on his skin, so different from the smooth touch of the typical men in my life. Men who wouldn't know a hammer from a wrench. I find a guy who works with his hands surprisingly sexy.

Especially this man. "Thank you," I say, clasping his hand in mine. "I know I pushed you into letting me stay and I'm truly grateful." Before I lose my nerve, I rise to my toes and press a lingering kiss to his cheek before spinning on my heels and walking away.

CHAPTER THREE

Maddox

I SPEND THE next few hours at the bar, catching up on paperwork and doing my best not to think about my new houseguest and those kisses. The one in my kitchen nearly had me throwing my common sense out the window and hauling her into my bed, and the sweet brush against my cheek shouldn't have impacted me the way it did. Both left me rock hard and wanting her, and appreciating her ability to be gracious even if she was right. She pushed me into the decision.

A knock sounds on the door, and I look up, grateful for the distraction. "Hey," I say, leaning back in my seat.

Zach walks into the room followed by Remy. Zach was the first man to start an investigative agency as well as the first Back Door in New York City. Once Remy left the police force, he bought into both businesses, and they opened the bar in the Hamptons.

What few people know, because he doesn't announce it, is that Remy, full name Remington Sterling, is one of *The* Sterlings, a family who owns a financial equity firm going back two generations. The man is incredibly wealthy but never acts like he comes from money. He has ghosts in his past he never speaks of, and I won't push. A man is entitled to his secrets. First a New York City detective, now a bar owner and P.I., Remy resides in Manhattan and keeps a low profile.

"To what do I owe the pleasure?" I ask my bosses.

It's not unusual for the men to come to the bar, but Zach usually leaves me to run things unless there are issues, like when my younger brother was stealing from the liquor supply. I still cringe at the memory. Luckily, neither man held it against me, and thanks in part to Zach's woman, Hadley, my brother got his life back on track. Remy and Zach go back and forth between the city and the Hamptons for business meetings with the Hamptons being the summer site of choice.

Zach settles into the chair in front of my desk. "Hadley wanted to go shopping and I figured I'd come see how you're doing. Ran into *him* as I was walking in." He gestures to Remy, who is leaning against the wall beside him.

"Everything at the bar is quiet, as in no issues," I assure them.

"Not here to check on you," Zach says. "We're both killing time until lunch."

Though I nod as if I understand my boss's life, I've given up on having a woman to share things with. While working in the city, making bank and mingling with the wealthy, women threw themselves at me. Even having a girlfriend didn't deter the more determined female. But I learned fast. I never knew if a woman was interested in me as a person or my money in the bank. My ex merely put the last nail in the coffin of relationships.

Once I returned to my working-class roots, I discovered the same kind of woman in the Hamptons wants to slum with a hot bar manager—not my words—but would never consider a man like me as a life partner. I'm jaded and don't want any woman for more than a night. Not everyone can have what my parents share.

I jolt with a start, realizing I drifted off in thought while Remy and Zach are discussing the New York Yankees and soon, all three of us segue into how football pre-season is starting soon.

"Knock knock," a familiar voice says, as Hadley strides in, her hair in a casual ponytail. No makeup, like Gabby. Apparently, Zach and I have the same type. *Wait. Fuck.* I shouldn't be thinking of Gabby as my type.

"Look who I found at the gallery."

As if my thoughts conjured her, Gabby strides in behind Hadley, holding a handful of shopping bags. She mentioned going shopping, and I assumed she'd pick up a few things to get by while she stayed with me. Apparently, figuring out her life includes spending lots of Daddy's money.

I narrow my gaze. "How do you know each other?" I stare at my houseguest, whose face is flushed and her eyes bright. Something has her excited, and I'm curious.

"We don't. I was in the gallery to apply for a job and Rhonda, the owner, went into the back to get an application—" Gabby begins, taking me off guard.

A job? Maybe I underestimated her determination to make choices and be on her own.

"And…" Hadley grins, happy to pick up the story. "I walked in to ask about a painting in the window. Gabby started telling me about the artist I was interested in. Then Rhonda returned—"

"And I had no idea she'd been listening, but she walked out and offered me a job on the spot!" Gabby drops her bags on the floor in front of her, walks up to where I sit behind my desk and throws her arms around my neck, hugging me tight. *"I got a job!"*

Her excitement is infectious, her squeal adorable, and her desire to share the news with me causes a surprising rush of happiness for her. Over her shoulder, I meet Zach's shocked stare. *Shit.* The last thing I want to do is answer questions about my relationship with Gabby. Hell, we don't have a relationship, and I've only known her for a day. Before I can peel her off me, she steps back.

"Congratulations," Remy says.

"Thank you!"

Hadley walks over to Zach, who has risen from his seat. He wraps an arm around her waist and pulls her in for a kiss that's awkward for everyone watching. These two are in love. After almost a decade apart and a lot of drama not long ago that brought Hadley back into his life, I understand their need to be close now.

After they end the kiss, Hadley glances from Gabby to Zach. "Gabby, this is my husband Zach, co-owner of this bar. And this is his partner, Remy Sterling."

Gabby laughs, her cheeks still flushed pink. "I assumed he was your…something after that kiss."

Hadley ducks her head. "We're still in the honeymoon phase of our relationship."

Gabby smiles and raises a hand in greeting. "Nice to meet you both."

They both nod, acknowledging her.

"That doesn't explain how you two ended up here together," I say, an eyebrow raised in curiosity.

Hadley shrugs. "When we walked out, we headed in the same direction. Again, we started talking and…here we are." She shoots me a concerned look. "Something wrong?"

I shake my head. I'm just overwhelmed by the whirlwind that is Gabrielle Davenport.

"Ready to go grab a bite?" Zach asks Hadley.

She nods. "Ready. Remy?"

He walks towards them. Like me, Remy is single but the three of them are a tight group. "Let's go get a table," Remy says, then turns, glancing at me. "How do you two know each other?" He glances between Gabby and me, with a smirk on his lips.

As I try to find the best explanation, Gabby answers for me. "I had some…personal issues, came to the bar, got a little too drunk and Maddox was nice enough to let me sleep at his place. I can't go home yet, so again, he's being such a gentleman letting me stay longer."

Both Zach's and Remy's eyebrows shoot upward.

I'm not sure if it was her calling me a gentleman or the fact that I have this young spitfire living with me. Temporarily, I remind myself. "It isn't for long, and she's in Joe's old room," I say of my brother.

"Isn't that what they all say?" Zach snickers, and Remy chuckles, enjoying putting me on the spot.

Hadley rolls her eyes. "I'm sorry they're behaving like adolescents," she says and turns her gaze to Gabby. "Congratulations again. You have my cell phone now. Call me and we'll have lunch or drinks."

"I'd love to!" Gabby smiles as the trio walks out the door, then she turns to me.

"Making friends, I see."

She braces her hands on her hips, tipping her head to one side. "Do you have an issue with that?"

Do I have an issue with her making friends with my people? Becoming even more a part of my world? Getting a job around the corner?

I have no fucking clue. "Congratulations on the job," I say instead of answering her.

"Thank you." She blows out a long, obviously relieved breath. "I didn't expect it, but I'm so excited. It's something I got on my own. I wanted to be a docent at a museum but that didn't happen."

"Why not?" I can't help but be curious about her.

She lifts her shoulders in a little shrug. "My parents, of course. I majored in art history and applied to the museums in Manhattan." Her eyes sparkle as she speaks, the idea obviously a passion of hers.

"What did they do?" I ask of her parents, already angry on Gabby's behalf.

"They interfered, what else? Both called their friends and contacts who are on the boards of the larger institutions. Everyone turned me down. One woman on the board of a smaller museum admitted she was afraid to lose my father's yearly donation."

Her dejected look doesn't sit well with me. Nobody deserves to have their dreams undermined by people who are supposed to love them.

"I didn't get one interview." Her normally sweet disposition gives way to a frown, and she curls her hands into fists at her side. "I had straight A's in my major. I paint and have taken classes for years, but do they care? Acknowledge my ability? No, they do not," she says, clearly on a roll and not waiting for a reply. "They want me to be a stay-at-home wife, be active on charity boards, and host dinners for my *hardworking* husband." She treats me to that cute wrinkle of her nose again. "As if I'd marry Mr. Grabby-hands." Her face flushes, this time not from anything good.

The reminder of how Preston cornered her has my own hands curling into fists. I'm not frustrated, I'm furious. Given the chance, I'd introduce the man's face to a wall and remind him what happens when he touches someone without consent.

I step forward and brace my hands on her shoulders. "Breathe, Gabby." I unintentionally hit a nerve with my question, and I want to calm her. "Hey. Be proud of what you *did* accomplish, okay? Forget about the past and concentrate on the present and the good things happening for you."

She nods, and when she glances up, I notice her eyes are wet. *Shit.* I hate when women cry. I grew up with a mom who never showed her sadness; she kept it hidden. I have a brother, not a sister. And the women I've dated specialized more in fake tears than real ones.

Something about Gabby gets to me, though. Her genuine personality and the vulnerability she doesn't hide shine through. I sense she's *real.*

And to a jaded guy like me, that trait is extremely appealing.

★ ★ ★

Maddox

A WEEK AFTER I told Gabby she could stay, I sit at my desk, staring at an inventory sheet. It's late, and numbers blur before my eyes so I rub them with my palms. I don't have to wonder what's on my mind. It's the same thing always in my head. My houseguest, who continues to surprise me, and not in a bad way.

Last week, after Gabby left the bar, I spent a couple of hours overseeing things at work and taking the time to convince myself I was prepared to have her living under my roof. The house isn't large, and I knew we were going to be in close quarters, so I needed to remind myself of all the reasons I should keep my hands to myself.

I thought I prepared myself to have Gabby in my home. At least that's what I told myself by the time I left work a few hours after she took her car home. *My* home, *not* hers. Unfortunately, it wasn't as easy as I convinced myself it would be.

Gabby is everywhere. Not only has she purchased new towels for her bathroom, she bought some for mine, too. Not that she was in my bedroom or the primary bath, but she said she assumed mine were as old as hers. Which is true. I haven't updated them for years. I never even thought about it. Now I have plush, comfortable towels when I get out of the shower. It might be a small thing to someone else, but to me, it showed a thoughtful side even if she used the money she took from the bank and refused my offer to pay her back.

A part of me wants to fault the rich girl for using her money to give herself more luxury than I have in my fixer-upper home, but she doesn't seem to be all about indulgence. She just seems to want to contribute in some way while she stays here. Her hours are shorter than mine, and when I come home, often between the day and night shift, there is dinner on the table or in the fridge waiting for me. Good meals she cooks herself, not ordered in or picked up. With groceries she purchases despite me leaving cash on the counter with a note to use it for house necessities.

Felicia didn't cook. She didn't know how, and she gave me a hard time over not hiring a chef when, at the time, I made the money to afford it. But Gabby is different, and I'm not enough of an asshole not to admit the difference. So I won't allow myself to fall back on the rich girl cliché. I have to give credit where it's due.

Gabby cooks, she cleans, she does laundry…and she paints. In the family room where I haven't finished priming the walls, she's set up an easel and canvas she apparently keeps in her car. And when she isn't working at the gallery, which she says she loves, I often find her with AirPods in her ears and a paint brush in her hand. From the little I see of her work, because she often covers her paintings with a sheet, she works with acrylics.

In essence, over the last week, she's taken over my house. And though I ought to mind and be annoyed by her presence, I like having her around. None of which convinces me that seducing a twenty-two-year-old woman is in my best interest. I still have plenty of reservations, which include not just her age and our life experience differences, but my uncertainty of where she'll live when the summer ends. I'm still guarding my emotions, but with every day that passes, Gabby makes that more difficult.

Shouting sounds from outside my office. Pushing back my chair, I rise to my feet. I'm not in the mood for a fight, but I'm grateful for the distraction from my thoughts. I walk out and stride down the hall, following the loud voices.

As I step foot in the bar, my gaze comes to rest on Cal who is in an argument with a familiar-looking man. I stride over to the douche in the pressed pants and a sport jacket, looking out of place in The Back Door where guys wear cargo shorts or jeans and T-shirts.

"Okay, Preston, what's the problem?" I shove my hands into my front pockets and glare.

The other man meets my gaze, clearly not surprised to see him. "James. I heard you were managing this dump." He scowls as he looks around the bar, which appears new and in great shape as far as I'm concerned. It just isn't the country club bar.

I ignore the dig. I don't give a shit what Preston the Third thinks of me or my occupation. "Why are you hassling my bartenders?"

I glance at Cal and tip my head toward the bar, indicating he can go back to work.

"Seems he's looking for his girlfriend." Cal shoots me a pointed look, one I accept with a nod.

After Cal returns to his place behind the bar and begins helping customers, I turn to Preston. "I wasn't aware you had a *girlfriend*. Women you touch without permission, on the other hand, I could count those, but it would take me all night."

"I'm not here to verbally spar with you. Where is she?"

"Where is who?" I deliberately play dumb. No way will I reveal Gabby's whereabouts. She is safely tucked away at my house and this prick won't find her.

Preston lets out a prolonged sigh, as if I'm

wasting his time. "Gabriella, my girlfriend. Soon to be fiancée."

"No idea who you're talking about." Though it's interesting to see how certain Preston appears that Gabby is his girlfriend and will bow to her family's demands.

"Gabriella has been missing for a week. Her parents and I were willing to give her time to get this little rebellion out of her system, but they've had enough. And so have I." He straightens his shoulders, posturing as if he has a leg to stand on.

Holding back a snort of amusement isn't easy, but I do it and remain silent.

"Do not make me call the police," Preston says, stepping closer. "My father has pull with the chief, and we both know who he'll believe. He'll come search your home, and no doubt he'll find my wayward fiancée."

I raise my eyebrows but still don't give the other man the satisfaction of a reply.

A growl of frustration escapes Preston's throat. "Gabriella's friends were here a few nights ago and saw her helping out behind the bar, talking to you and your workers. Or should I say slumming? You couldn't hack it in the world of finance so you tucked tail and came here."

Nothing the man says fazes me. Gabby's so-called friends betrayed her. Then again, on the first night we met, she told me she didn't have any friends she trusted. This just proves her instincts are solid.

And Preston is deluded in thinking she's his fiancée…or anything else. "You just said she was your girlfriend. Now you're claiming she's your fiancée. Even if you got your lies straight, we both know she's neither."

Preston's lips lift in a smug smile. "So you admit you know where she is?"

I fold my arms across my chest and glare at the man, barely holding onto my anger. "I know no such thing. Now get out of my bar, or I'll call for the bouncer and have *him* show you the door."

"And I'll call the police."

This asshole's posturing is getting old. "*Gabby*—" I emphasize her preferred name. "—is an adult, asshole. You can't make her do anything she doesn't want to do. Which brings me to another point." Stepping into Preston's personal space, I walk forward until I back the man against the bar, bracing my arm at his throat. Not to hurt but to make my point about the way he attacked Gabby. "If you ever put your hand on her or any other woman again and I find out about it, I'll put your pretty face through the nearest wall."

Preston's complexion grows pale. "You can't prove a damn thing."

"I don't need to. I've seen you in action, and I'd trust the word of any woman over a piece of shit like you." I drop my arm and step back. "I take it we have an understanding."

Preston shrugs and fixes his collared dress shirt. "Her parents will never allow her to walk away."

I snort. "You clearly don't know her very well. Now get the hell out of my bar before *I* call the cops."

Preston's cheeks turn red, and he spins on his dress shoes and walks away.

"What a dick," Cal says, coming up behind me.

I nod. "I'm leaving." I want to make sure Barrett doesn't figure out where Gabby is staying and make a stop on the way home.

I might have spent the last week avoiding the combination of minx, flirt, and innocent that is Gabby, but things have changed. Preston's appearance, trying to stake his claim, has me reevaluating what I want from my houseguest.

CHAPTER FOUR

Gabby

I YAWN. I stayed up watching a movie on television in the family room. The couch is comfortable, and once the walls are painted the warm cream, based on the samples already on the walls, combined with the wood trim, the room will have a homier feel.

I rise to my feet and walk into the kitchen where I pour a glass of water and finish the drink just as I hear the front door open and close again. My stomach flips at the sound.

Knowing Maddox is home, I can't deny the anticipation that courses through my veins. The week here has flown by. Staying at his house has worked out. He accepts my presence and though he keeps his distance, I feel him watching me when he thinks I'm not looking. I understand, because I'm always aware of him, sensing his presence before I know for sure that he's nearby.

More than once, I caught his heavy-lidded

gaze and hoped he was suffering with the same suppressed desire I am, knowing he was in his bedroom, a short walk across the house. Eventually, I gave in. I slipped my fingers into my shorts and stroked my wet sex. I pretended it was *his* fingers arousing me and sliding inside me. That it was *his* tongue on my clit as I came. And afterwards, as I caught my breath, my body pulsing but still somehow empty, I wondered if he was in his bedroom, masturbating while thinking of me.

"Gabby?"

His voice startles me despite hearing him come in. I place my glass in the sink before heading out of the kitchen and meeting up with him as he locks the front door.

"Hi," I say.

He turns, his gaze darkening as he takes in my bedtime outfit, a camisole and matching shorts. They're my favorite pair, decorated with pastel-colored stars on a white background. I thought I'd be in my room when he returned. Hadn't planned for him to see me in the barely-there pajama set, but I can't deny I like knowing my skimpy outfit affects him.

"Hey," he says in a gruff voice that causes goosebumps to pop out on my skin.

I clear my throat. "How was work?"

"Interesting. Had a customer asking Cal questions about you."

My eyes open wide, and my heart begins racing. "Who?" I can't imagine either of my parents showing up at The Back Door which leaves just one person, and the thought makes me nauseous.

"Preston Barrett, III. He came in making threats, posturing and claiming you were his girlfriend and then fiancée." Maddox's voice sounds low, pissed, and if I'm not mistaken, possessive.

"What did you do?" Worry tinges my voice, and my throat grows dry, making me wish for the water I left in the kitchen.

His expression softens as he meets my gaze. "I made sure he knew what would happen if he didn't learn that *no means no*. I also reminded him you weren't his girlfriend or his fiancée and he'd better leave you alone."

"Thank you." I breathe out the words, grateful for Maddox and his protection. "Does Preston know I'm staying here?"

He shakes his head. "But he knows you hang out at the bar."

He hesitates, obviously wanting to say more

but holding back, and I narrow my gaze. "What is it?" I ask.

He places one hand on my shoulder. "Apparently your *friends* were in the bar one night when you were there helping. They saw you and that's how Preston knew where to come looking."

I nod, and though I ought to feel betrayed, I never believed any of the girls in my social circles were my real friends. "Thanks for telling me, but I can't say I'm surprised."

He settles his free hand on my other shoulder, and I lean into his protective grasp. "You deserve better," he says in a husky voice. "You should have people in your life you can trust."

I swallow hard at the sincerity in his voice, pushing back the lump in my throat. It isn't often I let myself think about what I'm missing in my life. It wouldn't do me any good. My focus has always been on looking ahead and making sure I hold tight to whatever convictions I can. Like standing firm against my parents' desire for me to date and marry Preston.

"I have my grandmother. She knows where I am and she'd never say a word," I murmur. "I have my sister. And now I have you."

His eyes open wide, his surprise evident. I understand. I'm not sure what possessed me to include him in my tiny circle, but my gut tells me it's true. He gave me a place to stay, allows me to help at the bar he manages, lets me paint in his house, and most importantly, he kept Preston away. Not to mention, he threatened him on my behalf.

Yes, I can trust Maddox James.

I also want him. Want him to kiss me without reservation this time. Want to see his muscled, sexy body naked and aroused for me, and to feel his warmth on my skin.

I want him to take my virginity.

There is so much he can show me, teach me, and make me feel. Though I know, even if I convince Maddox to let himself go, this thing between us can only be temporary. He's already listed his reasons he isn't right for me.

Even if I know he's wrong.

Despite the obstacles, I won't be deterred. I meet his hooded gaze and see the desire in his eyes. He's feeling the same need.

"Maddox? Are you going to push me away again?" I ask in a whisper.

A long moment passes, and I wait, anxious and nervous. I can't handle another rejection, but I'll never regret putting myself out there. I sense he'll be worth it.

A low growl sounds from inside him, and he finally caves, lowering his head, his mouth inches from mine.

"I want you, Gabby."

My heart explodes with happiness, and with the feeling of déjà vu inside me, I rise onto my toes and press my lips against his, sliding my tongue inside his mouth. The hands on my shoulders moved to my hips and then he's lifting me without breaking the kiss. I wrap my legs around his waist, and somehow, he walks us through the house and toward his bedroom, stopping only to lay me down on the bed.

He leans over me and braces his arms on either side of my head. "And you're right. You *can* trust me."

I glance up at him and know I have to be honest. "Then you should know something before we go any further."

He presses his lips to mine, ignoring my words for a long kiss, one that almost has me forgetting what I need to say.

"What is it?" he asks as he rises and lifts the hem of his shirt, pulling it over his head, revealing the gorgeous, tanned chest I've dreamed about touching.

I hope my next words don't put an end to my daydreams.

"I'm a virgin."

★ ★ ★

Maddox

GABBY'S WORDS ECHO in my ears. "You're…what?" I shake my head. "Never mind. Stupid question. I heard you." I just can't believe it. I noticed her innocence in some things, but don't most women have sex in college?

"Surprise! I was waiting for the right man." Her cheeks flush pink in embarrassment, and she rolls to her side in an attempt to scramble off the bed.

I stop her, flipping her onto her back again. "Hold up. You didn't give me a chance to respond."

"Maybe I don't want to hear you tell me, *you're sorry but it's too much responsibility.*"

I blow out a rough breath. A smarter man would let her go. A man who wasn't feeling so protective of her would do the same. But I can't. Despite how fast it's happened, she's gotten under my skin. If anyone is going to be her first, it will be me. My age, experience, and our socio-economic differences be damned.

"You aren't too much responsibility. You're exactly the woman I want."

She blinks, her pretty green eyes and her expression holding a mix of surprise and pleasure. "That's quite a change from the man who said, *this kiss was a mistake.*"

"Because it wasn't." And I can't contain my grin because the other thing I enjoy is her mix of sweetness and sass.

"Good to know—" she starts to say.

I cut her off with a kiss. I slide my tongue between her lips and position myself on top of her once more, taking my time to devour her and learn every sweet inch of her mouth. With a moan, she slides her fingers through my hair and holds me in place, the kiss going on longer than I ever spent just making out. And not just because I want to make tonight good for her, which I do, but this moment means something to me, too.

Taking my time, I move away from her mouth and press slow kisses down her neck, along her collarbone, her body trembling with desire.

"I didn't know," she murmurs, her fingers still threading through my hair.

"What?"

She kisses my jaw, and my cock grows harder. "That my body had so many erogenous zones."

"It does. And I bet I can find more." Sliding my hands up her sides, I caress her soft skin, then grab the hem of the flimsy camisole, lift it over her head, and toss the garment onto the floor.

I lean back and take in her body, the curves of her breasts fuller than I realized, her nipples a dusky pink and hard, just begging for me to suck. That's what I do. At the first lick, Gabby sighs, and when I pull one into my mouth, she moans, her entire body writhing beneath me. With my other hand, I plump and caressed her other breast, rolling her nipple between my thumb and forefinger.

She arches her hips, and I know if I slip my hand beneath those loose shorts I'll find she's wet. Ready for me? Not yet, and I want to make this as easy for her as possible. I also need to find a way to keep myself under control because everything about her turns me on. Reining myself in won't be easy, but for her, I'll do it.

★　★　★

Gabby

MADDOX SEEMS TO know all the right spots to lick, suck, and yes, bite, I think, as my body hums in ways I never felt before. Did I make out with boys? Yes. And that's what they were. Boys. Maddox is all man, and the attention he gives to my body proves he isn't a selfish one, either.

He rises to his feet and strips off his pants. I take in his thick, heavy cock, obviously aroused, and my eyes open wide. I might be wet, but I don't know how he'll fit.

"Relax, princess. I'll make it good for you."

At his gruff words, warmth spreads like liquid through my veins. I believe him and reach down, wriggling off my shorts, taking my skimpy bikini underwear off with them.

Though inexperienced with sex, I don't want to make him feel like he's with a young girl, not when he's already made my age an issue. So, I bare myself to him, doing my best not to blush or attempt to cover myself. Instead, I lay down, as ready as I'll ever be. No matter how nervous I am, my sex throbs and feels empty. For the first time, I know what it's like to want. I want to be filled by him, even if it hurts.

"Fucking beautiful," he says, his hot gaze raking over my skin.

I swallow hard, aware of my nipples puckering even more under his approving stare. "Do you know what I've been thinking about since the first time I saw you without a shirt?" I ask, looking up into his handsome face.

"Tell me." He braces his hands on either side of my shoulders again, but this time, when he lowers himself, his hot erection pulses against my belly and my sex.

"I wanted to lick that tattoo on your shoulder," I admit, pushing myself to my elbows and doing just that, my tongue swiping across his hot skin. "Salty," I say. "And you smell good."

A light coating of precome smears across my stomach. Obviously, he likes that, so I continue, trailing a path along the tribal band.

"Enough." His gruff voice doesn't put me off, not when he's so hard and his hips arching against my body.

He draws a long breath. "I need to see if I have condoms," he mutters.

I ask myself if I trust him enough and decide yes, I do. "I'm on birth control, and you already know I've never done this before. How about you? Are you safe?"

"You're asking me if I can take you bare?" His gaze darkens at the rhetorical question. "I was tested after I left New York. I wasn't sure I trusted the woman I'd been with. Then did it again after…well, we can talk about it another time. I don't want anyone else between us right now."

I nod in understanding. "Then let's do this."

He shakes his head and chuckles. "You always surprise me. We're not just going to do this. I'm going to make sure you're so ready for me, nothing else matters."

He then slides down my body and sits between my thighs, his body resting on his knees. Gripping my thighs, he pulls my legs apart. "Put them on my shoulders."

No one has ever gone down on me, either, but I don't think this is the time to mention it. All too aware of his sizzling gaze on my nearly bare sex, I do as he instructs. But I can't watch any longer, and as his face draws closer, I shut my eyes in time for the first swipe of his tongue on my clit.

My hips buck, and I moan, the sound escaping because I never imagined how good this could feel.

"You taste delicious," he mutters and begins to suck and nibble, pulling my outer lips into his mouth, teasing me by licking me everywhere but where I need him most. He slides that talented tongue over the seam between my thigh and my sex, showing me yet another erogenous zone.

My pussy throbs with desire, and I begin to rock my hips, grinding myself against his mouth but not getting the friction I need. Suddenly he sucks my clit between his lips, and a flash fire rips through me.

"Maddox, please, more. Right there." I arch into him.

He grasps onto my hips, holding tight as he eats me like he can't get enough. I begin to spiral, rocking against his face until my climax hits, and I scream his name, stars flashing in front of my closed eyes as he takes me through the orgasm with continued licks and nibbles until I can't take it any longer.

"Enough, please." I lower my legs off his shoulders and open my eyes in time to see him lift his head and wipe his mouth on my thigh.

"I think you're ready," he says in a husky

voice that arouses me again.

And here I thought I was finished.

He crawls up my body until the head of his cock settles at my entrance. "I've got you," he promises, slowly pushing his way inside me.

He's right; I'm ready as he easily slips inside me a little bit, then another inch more. "Okay?" he asks.

I manage a nod though I feel stretched to the limit and unsure I can take any more of him. He captures my lips with his and kisses me, devouring my mouth until I can't think of anything but him. My hips rock against him, and without warning, he arches his hips and thrusts in deep, causing me to cry out in pain.

He lifts his head. "Shh. It'll get better. I promise."

Despite the tear that falls from my eye, I nod, trusting him.

Dipping his head, he licks my nipple, pulling it into his mouth and teasing with his teeth. Desire rushes through me, and he begins to move, rocking his hips against me before he slides out slowly, then pushes back in. He moves back up and kisses me again, picking up rhythm as he begins to pump into me.

"You're tight and feel so good."

His words sweep over me, and suddenly, I'm wet and taking all of him, arousal and pleasure combining into a heady mix.

"Okay?" he asks, looking deep into my eyes.

God, he's gorgeous and sexy, and so concerned about me it brings more tears to my eyes as I nod.

"Better than okay. Amazing."

His lips lift, and satisfaction gleams in his eyes. He pulls his hips back and thrusts in, repeating the action, his gaze never leaving mine. I have the sense he's making sure he doesn't hurt me.

He can't. Not anymore.

"Harder, Maddox. And don't stop."

He complies, pounding into me, and my body responds, waves of pleasure rocking through me, rising with each successive thrust.

"I'm not going to last," he says, shifting positions and suddenly hitting a spot inside me that feels incredible.

"There. Again." He repeats the motion and a rush of arousal sweeps me up and over the edge. "Maddox, oh God, I'm coming." Nothing has ever felt as good.

He loses that control he's been holding onto, and his thrusts become harder, rougher, less coordinated. "Fuck, princess, yes." He follows me over with a long groan that I feel down to my soul.

CHAPTER FIVE

Maddox

I WAKE UP, a warm, soft body lying in the crook of my arm and cuddling against my body. It takes a few seconds for me to remember what's going on, and once I do, I let out a long breath and talk to myself. I knew what I was getting into with Gabby. She was honest before we had sex, and everything in me wanted to be her first. It wasn't sex with a virgin that was throwing me off balance nor is it her age.

No, it's the intensity of our connection that has my head spinning. For a man who decided I was finished with relationships, I want more with Gabby. And no one else. Closing my eyes, I turn my head and breathe in the strawberry scent clinging to her hair, and my dick perks up. It is way more than morning wood where even my hand would do. I want to feel her tight walls around me again. I want to come, knowing we're in sync.

Since I know she'll be sore, I carefully move

my shoulder, letting her head come to rest on a pillow. I turn and look at her peaceful expression. She's so damned pretty, her makeup-free face and creamy complexion another thing I find appealing about her. The women I used to sleep with woke up before me to fix themselves before I got a glimpse of the real person beneath the heavy coverage. Until Gabby, I never realized how much I prefer the natural look, or how hard it could make me.

Her eyelids open, her long lashes fluttering as awareness hits her, and she looks at me with trepidation in her gaze. She's silent, assessing me. I have no doubt she wonders where my head is after last night.

"Morning, beautiful." I have no intention of leaving her hanging. I'm in this, willing to see where this relationship takes us, though I'm well aware she could still end up changing her mind and going home to her reality at any point in time.

A happy smile lifts her lips. "Good morning."

"How did you sleep?" I ask.

"Fantastic." She lifts her arms over her head and stretches, causing the covers to fall and her bare breasts to reveal themselves. "Oops!" She reaches for the top sheet, and I stop her.

"Nope. I like looking at you."

"You do?" Her cheeks flush pink.

I prop myself up on one elbow, lean over and press my mouth to hers, taking my time and enjoying, my tongue sliding against hers. She moans, hooking her arm around my neck.

"No regrets?" she asks, breaking the kiss.

I cock an eyebrow. "Shouldn't I be asking you that?" I lean back against the pillows, and she curls up against me.

"I wasn't the one who had issues with *us* to begin with."

Aah. She doesn't want to face me, still worried I'll change my mind. "Look at me."

She sighs and pushes herself to a sitting position. "Yes?"

Reaching out, I slide a piece of hair off her forehead and tuck it behind her ear. "One, we discussed that last night. Two, once I make up my mind, I don't change it without good reason, and three? You waited for the right man to give your virginity to." I cup her chin in my hand. "Am I still that right man?"

She nods. "No regrets."

"Good. Me, neither. Now, give me another kiss, we'll shower, and I'll take you out for breakfast."

She leans forward on her knees and crawls toward me, arching her back and kissing me with everything in her. I groan and pull her against me, her curvy body coming to rest on top of me.

"What happened to the shower?" she asks, wriggling her hips and grinding her sex into my hard cock.

I cup her ass cheeks in my hands and squeeze. "Are you feeling up for a second round, or are you sore? I can draw a bath—"

Her eyes soften. "Look at this new side of you. I had no idea you could be…sweet."

"What can I say? You bring out that dormant side of me."

Her eyes open wide, and she scrambles to a sitting position, her wet sex covering my lower abdomen and I think I'll explode.

"Dormant means you were softer at one point and then you changed. What did Wall Street do to you?" she asks, obviously determined to talk.

Having a conversation is the last thing I want to do, but I resign myself to being horny and uncomfortable while we talk. "More like what did the women in that world do to me?"

Gabby wrinkles her nose. "What was her name?"

"Felicia. But it started before her. My parents are good people. Dad's an electrician and Mom stayed home with me and my younger brother. We didn't have a lot but we had enough. And we were happy. But I got a scholarship to Columbia and then got my MBA. Before I knew it, I was on Wall Street and mingling with people I never thought I'd meet. Not given how I'd grown up." And that is a mouthful more than I ever planned to reveal.

"People like me? My family? Preston?" she asks.

I sigh. "You're nothing like them."

"But you thought I was. When you met me at the bar, right? Tell me. I won't be angry."

I nod. "I did, at first. Then you showed up the next day with a job and towels for the guest bathroom and for mine. Next thing I knew, you were working in the mornings, painting in the afternoons, coming to the bar at night and helping out by clearing dirty glasses." I shake my head and grin. "Blew my initial perception of you out of the water."

"I live to shock you," she says wryly. "I take it you *liked* what you saw?"

I nod. "More than liked. I admired you. In one short week, you changed what I thought of you and I stopped fighting my desire."

"Lucky me," she whispers.

Finally, I think, we can move on from talking. I reach for her breast, and she arches backward. "Tell me about Felicia."

I groan. "Seriously? We're both naked, and you want to hear about my ex?"

She shakes her head. "I want to learn more about *you*." She places a hand on my chest, over my heart.

I can't deny her. And once I tell her everything, we can move on to better things. "Okay. I met a woman at one of the fundraising events I went to on behalf of the firm. We dated and pretty much lived together. She looked good as my date and I convinced myself I cared for her but I know better now."

"What changed?" Gabby asks, her gaze soft on mine.

"I hated the people I worked with, disliked the pretentiousness surrounding me. I'd already made enough money to put it in savings and do what would make me happy." I lift my shoulders in a shrug. "I didn't know what that was at the time but I saw this house advertised. It was rundown and needed renovations and it called to me. So I bought it and moved here."

She looks around the bedroom that still needs massive painting and work. "I like it, too. I can envision the entire house when it's finished. It'll be a *home*." Her lips curl up in a smile, and I want nothing more than to kiss her.

She pats my chest. "Go on. I want to hear it all."

I roll my eyes. "You're a bossy thing. Okay, fine. I began the reno process. One night I met Zach and Remy at The Back Door and offered up my bartending services. I worked evenings for a couple of months and enjoyed it. Eventually, Remy had to go back to the city to the Manhattan bar, and they promoted me to manager." I shrug. "The casual, easy lifestyle works for me."

"Thank you. I know you weren't in the mood to revisit the past."

"I don't mind telling you." And I don't. She listens and understands me on a level that shocks me, given she comes from the world I've been so disillusioned with.

"How about that shower?"

She climbs off me, and a cool chill rushes over my skin.

"You go first. If we shower together, I'll forget you need some time to recuperate before we go again."

"Tonight," she says, and my cock hardens at the promise in her words.

I nod. "Tonight," I agree.

"I'm going to use the other bathroom. All my stuff is in there." She walks out of the room naked, more comfortable with her nudity around me than I expect.

She'll be at least twenty minutes in the shower, and I don't want to tempt fate by us both using the hot water at the same time. I could use a cup of coffee. I rise to my feet and pull on my track pants, walking to the kitchen.

No sooner have I pulled out a K-cup than my doorbell rings. I'm not expecting company.

I stride to my door and look through the glass. An older woman stands outside, leaning on a brightly decorated cane. Her hair is blonde with light streaks of gray, and she wears long sleeves in ninety-degree weather, a pair of pressed slacks and sneakers, no doubt for better balance. On the street behind her, a black Lincoln Town Car with a driver appears to idle.

I glance at her face. The moment I take in her emerald-green eyes, I know who she is and open the door. "You must be Gabby's grandmother."

"What gave me away?" she asks. "My good looks?"

I grin, liking this woman already. "Your eyes. Come in." I have no doubt Gabby will want to see her grandmother. She was the first person mentioned when she listed who she could trust.

But what if she wants Gabby to return home? Will she be swayed by the woman she adores? A pang gnaws at my gut, but I push it aside. Gabby has the right to make her own choices, and I have to respect them. Even if somehow, I've done a one-eighty and want her to stay.

I grasp the older woman's free arm and lead her to the kitchen. "Have a seat. Can I make you a cup of coffee?"

She lowers herself into a chair, leaning her cane against the table. "No, thank you. The doctors are worried about my blood pressure and have me cutting back on caffeine. I'd sneak it but I can't risk dying and leaving Gabriella alone with her parents. It's a pity my son turned into such a social climber." She tsks. "I see those wide eyes. You're shocked. Gabriella didn't tell you about me? I say what I think. To anyone."

I try my damnedest not to grin but lose the battle. "She told me you're one of the only people she trusts. That alone made me like you but now I see where Gabby gets her easy-going personality. She's lucky to have you, Mrs. Davenport."

"Annabelle. Don't make me look over my shoulder to see if my mother-in-law came back from the grave."

I bite the inside of my cheek. "Annabelle. Gabby's in the shower. I'm sure she'll be out soon, and she'll be happy you're here." I pause. "Why *are* you here? Just to see your granddaughter?" I can't hold back the question plaguing me.

"I'm here to see if you're good enough for my Gabriella."

She catches me mid-swallow, and I cough. "Excuse me?"

She grins, and I see glimpses of Gabby in her expression. "My other granddaughter, Penelope, who I love dearly but could never convince to be her own person, keeps in touch with her sister. I'm well aware Gabriella has feelings for you. So tell me, why should I approve of you?"

"Grandmother!" Gabby walks into the

kitchen and strides over to Annabelle. "What are you doing here and why are you grilling the man nice enough to give me a place to stay?"

Annabelle uses the table to push herself up until she stands. "I'm here because I missed seeing your face." She hugs Gabby, and Gabby squeezes her tight.

I'm glad she has this woman in her life.

"Besides, someone has to judge this man before you two really start living in sin."

Before I can worry she's serious, she lets out a laugh and winks at me. Then she sits back down.

"Good job, Gabriella. He's good-looking and I can tell he's got muscles." She turns my way. "Now tell me about yourself, Maddox."

I shoot Gabby an amused look and with a resigned sigh, Gabby seats herself into the chair next to her grandmother. "Just give her the highlights," she whispers.

"No, I want all the dirty details." She props her chin in her hand and smiles at me.

And at that moment, I know I already have the older woman's approval. For reasons I've yet to fathom, that means something to me.

★　★　★

Gabby

AN HOUR LATER, I decide that Maddox is my grandmother's newest best friend. Annabelle grills him like the professional busybody she is and to my surprise, Maddox fills her in on his entire life. No matter how many times I insist he does not have to answer, he and my grandmother ignore me, chatting like old friends. She even fills him in about the love story between Annabelle and Maximillian, her husband and my grandfather.

Unlike my parents, who married each other for wealth and status, Annabelle and Max were deeply in love before he died about ten years ago. Which is the reason my grandmother wants the same for me, who she thinks is very much like her younger self. Watching the two people I care about getting to know one another warms my heart. It tells me that my instincts about Maddox are spot on. He's a good man who has patience for an older woman…because she's my grandmother.

A honk sounds from outside, and Annabelle frowns. "That's my cue. Harold is getting impatient," she says of her long-time driver.

Maddox rises and lifts Annabelle's cane, then helps her to stand.

"A gentleman." She nods in approval and steps over to him. "I like you, Mr. James."

She pats his cheek and when she lowers her arm, he clasps her weathered hand in his. "I don't know what the future holds, Annabelle, but you can trust your granddaughter with me."

My stomach does a flip as he mentions the future. Although the romance novel reader in me wants to believe in happily-ever-after, I know I have to be pragmatic. We've only known one another for a week. Despite my rapidly beating heart, I can't assume forever is in the cards. But I want to get to know him better and stick around while we build...*something* together.

"Gabriella." My grandmother crooks her finger and I step closer. Annabelle pulls an envelope out of her purse. "Use this for anything you need while you get yourself settled. And call me if you need *anything.*"

My eyes fill with tears at the sweet gesture. "Thank you, but I can't take your money."

I feel the heat of Maddox's stare as my grandma and I talk. He's already told me how he views wealthy women, but that isn't why I'm turning down the gift. "I need to stand on my own and not rely on my trust fund or you. But I love you for the offer."

"Keep it as your safety net," Annabelle insists. "Your father has cut you off." She frowns at that fact.

Though I know I've been all but disinherited for my rebellion, hearing it hurts just the same.

To my surprise, Maddox steps up behind me, wraps an arm around my waist and kisses the top of my head. As if he's in tune with my emotions…and he probably is. I step back, my body leaning against his. I don't need his strength, I could handle things on my own, but I appreciate it anyway. He cares, and my heart flutters in my chest.

"Have my parents been pressuring you about asking me to come home?" I ask. No doubt they assume I'd keep in touch with my grandmother.

Annabelle shakes her head. "I've heard them talking though. They assume you'll tire of this independent stand you're taking and come home."

Behind me, Maddox stiffens. He probably

worries about the same thing. Only time will prove I'm here to stay. With or without Maddox, I'm building a life of my own.

"Listen," my grandmother says. "You have the car because I bought it for you and the title is in your name. Your father can't take the vehicle from you. When you come back to the city, for whatever reason, call me. We'll meet with the lawyers and move your trust fund somewhere your father won't know about it. I think we'll both feel better."

Eyes stinging, I nod.

"Now keep the money. Open an account here. And we'll talk. I love you, dear girl."

"I love you, too," I whisper, hugging her tight.

The car horn blares again.

"Come on. I'll walk you out," Maddox says, hooking an arm through Annabelle's.

I wait in the kitchen, watching through the window, my thoughts on Maddox and the night we spent together. I never had sex before. Never slept in the same bed with a guy overnight. And I've never felt cared for, safe or protected by a man, either.

Until Maddox.

I gave him my virginity with no strings, but

with everything inside me, I want to hold on tight and create more lasting bonds with this special man.

CHAPTER SIX

Gabby

M Y PHONE RINGS, startling me. I've been lost in my painting world, splattering glorious bold colors onto the paper. With my hands a mess and my brush in hand, I ignore the call but when the cell rings again, I wipe my dirty fingers on a rag and carefully lift the phone.

Rhonda's name flashes on the screen. I left the gallery when my shift ended earlier and came home to paint.

"Hello? Rhonda? Is everything okay? Do you need me to come back in?" I ask.

"Nothing's wrong. I have the most exciting news. Your first painting sold!"

I scream. "Oh my God! That's amazing!"

Rhonda chuckles. "Wait until you hear for how much." She told Gabby a number that blew her mind. "Now go celebrate!"

I disconnect, my heart pounding in excitement. In the two weeks during which I've worked there, I found myself confiding in my boss. We discuss everything. I admitted why I left my parents' home and my need to apply for a job to make money of my own. We talked about my degree, museums and the fact that I am a closet painter, hiding my work from my parents. The first time my mother caught me with dirty fingernails, she forbade me from indulging in my *frivolous hobby*.

Rhonda convinced me to bring some pieces by the gallery for her to see, and my sister took a day trip from her Long Island home to drop off canvases I already painted and stored in Penelope's basement. Rhonda fell in love with my work. I would have thought my boss was being kind, except Rhonda never hangs anything in her place of business she doesn't believe in. The next day, my modern contemporary art was framed and hanging in a small corner.

And today it sold.

I run for the bathroom and take a quick shower, aware I can't get rid of all the paint on my hands but knowing Maddox won't mind. Smiling at the thought, I dress in a pair of fitted black running shorts, a purple sport bra, and a lightweight jacket. Casual clothes I like wearing when not working or painting.

After grabbing my keys, I rush to my car, turned on the engine and drive toward town. Although I'll share my news with my grandmother and Penelope later, Maddox is the first person I want to celebrate with.

I've been staying with him for a total of three weeks and things between us have been…almost perfect. From the routine we fell into as a couple to how in sync we are when it comes to music, action-adventure movies, and documentaries on television. Neither of us is overly attached to social media, me because I don't have friends I want to check up on, and Maddox only looks out for his younger brother and the business page for the bar.

If only I didn't catch him deep in thought on a few occasions. Sometimes I walk into the kitchen and find him staring out the window or on the terrace, looking out at the horizon. I have to call his name a few times before it registers I'm speaking to him. Those moments make me wonder what's bothering him. Am I suffocating him by living in his house…and now sharing his bed?

Yet, it's hard to imagine he feels smothered when he can't get enough of me. He often wakes me with his mouth on my sex, his tongue almost bringing me to orgasm before I register it isn't an erotic dream. Once I'm awake, he finishes the job, making me scream his name as glorious bliss overcomes me.

At night, I'm only too happy to return the favor, and I try, but he always pulls his cock out of my mouth, refusing to come down my throat when *he needs to be inside me when he comes.* His words, ones that I take to heart.

Maddox also taught me new positions, and I have to admit I have two favorites. Sitting over his face while he devours my pussy and makes me come with his tongue licking my clit. And after, he positions me on my hands and knees and slams into me from behind, hitting that elusive G-spot and causing me to see stars as my orgasm shakes my world.

But my ultimate favorite sexual thing between us happened this morning. And it's what convinces me Maddox is as invested in our relationship as I am. Instead of waking me with his mouth, I came to with his warm body on top of mine and his cock poised at my entrance. Once I was awake, he slid into me ever so slowly, gliding in and out, his chocolate-brown gaze never leaving mine. In his eyes, I saw warmth and caring mixing together as our bodies connected.

Then, he pulled me to a sitting position, his legs bent beneath him and positioned my legs on either side of his body. Still joined, he was as deep as possible inside me, filling me so there was no way to tell where he ended, and I began. We were one as he began to lift his hips and I rocked in unison to his movements.

He held my stare, refusing to let me look away as we built higher and higher, climaxing at the same time. I have no doubt he made love to me and felt the emotions rushing through me. His awed expression revealed his raw emotions, too.

But I'm still young, still naïve when it comes to men, and I'm trusting him not to hurt me and believing in what I see.

Which is why I wonder if those off-moments are about something else. He mentioned our many differences, but I think living together proves how compatible we are. Besides, his lost-in-thought moments began after my grandmother left.

After I asked Annabelle about my parents and my grandmother replied, *they assume you'll tire of this independent stand you're taking and come home.*

That comment caused Maddox to stiffen and pull into himself before he walked Anabelle to her car.

I don't know and haven't pushed him for answers but maybe I should. Holding things in can't be healthy for a relationship. Penelope told me as much when I confided in my older sister.

I pull into the lot for The Back Door. It's nearing cocktail hour and both the dinner area and the bar tables are full.

I pause by the hostess stand. "Hi, Sheila."

"Hi, Gabby." The hostess, menus in hand, smiles at me, then leads a couple to one of the only empty tables, and I proceed to walk to the bar.

A heavy crowd fills up the space. Cal, Eddie and Vanna, another bartender I met in the last few weeks, are all working. Before I check out the office, looking for Maddox, I stop at the bar entrance.

"Vanna, have you seen Maddox?" I call out.

"He's sitting over there." The bartender, a cute woman with short spikey hair topped with pink, tips her head toward a cocktail table where Maddox is, along with the owners, Zach and Remy.

I nod. "Thanks." I start through the crowd, making my way to the table where they all sit.

Maddox catches sight of me first, a genuine grin lifts his lips, relieving my earlier anxiety.

With that worry out of the way for now, my excitement returns and I quicken my step. "Guess what?" I ask before I even reach him, unable to wait.

"Tell me." He rises to greet me.

My gaze sweeps over him, once again knocked on my butt by how well-built and sexy he is. And from the way he stares at me approvingly, I know he's all mine, and I push my worries aside.

"The gallery sold one of my paintings!" Without waiting, I throw my arms around his neck and he returns my hug, lifting me off the ground as he embraces me.

"I'm so damn proud of you," he says, his voice husky and gruff in my ear. "I knew you could do it."

At his words, my heart slams hard inside my chest. It isn't that I need his approval but receiving it from anyone is rare. Sure, my grandmother always gives her blessing. Annabelle loves me and would do anything to compensate for my parents' lack of caring and support. But coming from Maddox, as with Rhonda, I *know* the sentiment is genuine.

Rhonda thinks I have talent.

Maddox believes in me and that means *everything.*

"When I heard we could find you here, I didn't believe it," a familiar and unwelcome voice says.

I jerk in surprise and my stomach twists with dread.

"My mother," I whisper in Maddox's ear.

He doesn't release me or react, doesn't allow me to jump back and put distance between us, not that I'd try. He slides me down his body, letting me feel his strength, keeping one arm firmly around my waist.

I draw a deep breath and turn to see my parents, along with Preston and my grandmother, standing in front of us.

Maddox draws me more firmly to his side, staking his claim and being in my corner. It's all I've ever wanted from someone important in my life, and here he is, sensing my need and stepping up to provide it.

This is it. Time to stand up for myself, or my life will never be my own.

Since Preston's visit to the bar, my parents

turned suspiciously silent. No more voicemails or texts. I had a feeling they were biding their time until ready to strike. I tried to convince myself that I was ready for any upcoming confrontation. After all, what more could they do to hurt me? They already cut me off financially, and there was no emotional connection in any of my childhood memories.

I pull my shoulders back, facing my mother. My father stands by his wife's side while my grandmother leans on her colorful cane, no doubt waiting for the fireworks. Annabelle winks at me, confirming my suspicions.

"Who told you where I was?" I ask my parents, then turn my gaze to Preston. "Was it you?"

"It doesn't matter." My father lets out a huff of annoyance. "What does matter is that the entire country club is talking about you slumming at this bar, cleaning dirty glasses and serving alcohol." The disgust in his tone is evident.

Maddox grips me tighter but remains silent. He's trusting me to handle things, and I'm grateful.

"The only thing *that* tells me is someone in your crowd was here too, which makes any comment about this establishment hypocriti-cal," I say.

My father takes one step forward, but Mad-dox puts a hand out, stopping him from moving closer. My father clenches his jaw but doesn't say a word to him. Yet. No doubt his judgment is coming.

"What are you wearing in public?" my mother asks, her eyes wide, lips parted, her expression horrified.

I glance down and shrug. "Clothes."

"Workout clothes," Annabelle adds. "Don't you keep up with trends, Madeline?"

"Mother!" Aaron snaps. "Stay out of this. Now, Gabriella, we're leaving tonight and you're coming with us."

I blink in surprise. "You usually stay for the season. Why are you leaving when your summer isn't over?"

"Preston isn't leaving, we are. But he want-ed to be here. We are all tired of this rebellious phase. It's gone on long enough. Playing house with this…this…" My father stumbles over his words to describe Maddox.

"Bar manager and independent contractor?" I deliberately needle my parents with words they'll find cringeworthy. "Oh, and I wonder if

Preston mentioned that Maddox used to work on Wall Street? I believe you know of my father, Aaron Davenport, right, Maddox?"

Preston narrows his gaze but smartly remains silent.

I glance up at Maddox, hoping he knows I'm doing this performance for myself, yes but also for *us*. After this, my parents will leave me alone and that is exactly what I want.

"Yes." Maddox nods. "I used to work at Preston Barrett Jr.'s firm." He doesn't elaborate further, nor do I need him to.

My father stares, assessing Maddox. "It doesn't matter what he does for a living. You are not going to continue living with him." He turns his angry gaze on me. "Yes, I heard that, too. And I won't have it. I'm not funding this vacation." My father's voice rises, and people around us turn to watch.

My face burns with embarrassment, but I'm determined to see this through. "I don't need your money. You cut me off weeks ago, and I've done just fine."

"You cannot make enough money cleaning up at this bar to live in the Hamptons," my mother says, her blue eyes staring at me, daring me to disagree.

Madeline is in for a shock. "Then it's a good thing I have a job at the gallery since my work here is for free. I help out when things are busy."

Maddox squeezes my waist. Tipping his head, he whispers, "We'll need to get you on the books."

I stifle a laugh at his timing.

"But…" My mother pauses, caught off guard, then seems to collect herself. "Even gallery work won't keep you in the lifestyle you're accustomed to, Gabriella."

"Then it's a good thing I don't want that life."

My mother waves a dismissive hand. "That's easy to say now."

Preston turns to my mother. "Don't worry. Give her more time and she'll change her mind when she gets tired of living like a peasant."

I shake my head. "You are such an ass. And I won't grow tired of anything." None of them ever understood me at all. "*I'm happy here.* I love living with Maddox in his house." I pretty much love the man but don't think he's ready to hear those words after not quite one month.

But I reach back and squeeze his hand before continuing. "For once, I have the freedom to paint, to wear whatever I want…" I shrug off the cardigan, leaving myself in my shorts and sports bra, to the utter horror of my mother, whose mouth gapes open. "And it feels good to help at the bar and work at the gallery." This next part isn't as easy, but it's true. "And even if Maddox and I aren't together for the long term, though I hope we are, *I'm not leaving* the Hamptons." Or the man unless he insists, but that discussion is for us, alone. "In other words, Mother, Father, you can all go home without me."

Madeline gasps, probably more for effect. "I raised you better than to talk to us in that tone." She sniffles but again, it isn't real. "Mark my words, you will come back eventually, and you'll be lucky if someone in our social circle is willing to have you."

I sigh. "I'm not changing my mind, but only time will prove that to you." I pull in a deep breath. "Oh. And the best news of the night? My paintings are hanging in the gallery in town. In fact, I sold my first one today. So I'm more than certain I'll survive on my own."

My grandmother starts to clap, and though I grin, I shake my head. "One more thing. You are my parents, and though I may not like your views or beliefs you *are* my family. You know where I am if you ever want a *normal,* parent-child relationship. One where you accept me for who I am." I slide my hand into Maddox's and he grasps mine tight. "And who I choose to be with."

I ignore Preston. He isn't worth another breath.

The little girl who always wanted her parents to just *be her parents* and not wardens with rules and expectations hopes they will come around. But the adult me isn't counting on them to change. I'll always have my grandmother and Penelope. With a little luck, Maddox and I will have a future.

My grandmother claps in earnest, and my father huffs, his shoulders stiff.

"Let's go, Aaron." My mother's cheeks are flushed with anger.

"Have a good trip back to the city." Maddox speaks. "And don't worry about your daughter." Without warning, he bends his knees and picks me up, tossing me over his shoulder in a fireman's hold. "She's in good hands."

I let out a shriek but I really don't mind. And in case he's worried, I squeeze his ass hard.

"Aaron!" my mother yells. "Get me out of here."

"You always were a prude, Madeline," my grandmother says.

I let out a laugh at my grandmother's antics and the entire bar breaks out in applause that could have been in reaction to Maddox's caveman routine or my grandmother's comment. No matter, my family is in for a long ride home, I think, suddenly feeling the jolt of Maddox moving.

I grab onto a belt loop in his jeans, trying to ignore my stomach digging into his shoulder as he walks through the room. Though I can't see more than his delectable ass, a glance to the side reveals we're headed to his office.

And since he's carrying me away for the whole bar to see…I am holding out hope whatever he has to say will bode well for my future.

★   ★   ★

Maddox

GABBY'S PARENTS ARE pieces of work, I think, ignoring the clapping, as I stride through the crowd that parts for me. It's a wonder Gabby turned out as sweet and caring as she did. I suppose I have Annabelle to thank. That and some innate combination of sweetness and a core of steel inside my girl. One that made her willing to defy expectations and grow into her own person.

I didn't mean to make a scene. That isn't my style. But after listening to Gabby stand up to the people who raised her, I want one thing. To get her alone and assure her that yes, I'm in it for the long term, too. And I'm not letting her go.

I step into the office behind the bar and kick the door closed behind me, shutting out the noise. I have one hand around the back of her knees and the other on her ass which I can't *not* squeeze. Especially since she wears a skimpy Lycra outfit that outlines her curves and has me drooling.

"Hey! Are you going to put me down?" she asks. I still feel her finger curled into my belt loop.

"Do I have to?"

We haven't been together long, but I've spent most of our time together telling myself I can handle it if she decides to leave, but knowing I'm lying to myself. Now that she's announced her decision to stay, I want to keep her close.

But I lower her to her feet, holding onto her shoulders, steadying her.

She tips her head up to meet my gaze. And when I look into those gorgeous green eyes, I finally feel like I can breathe.

"Do you have any idea how amazing you are?" I ask.

Her eyes open wide, and her lips part in surprise. "Seriously? Why would you say that?"

How can she not know? "You stood up to your parents and that took courage. You took control of your life and that makes you brave. All in all, you're amazing."

Her smile lights up the room *and* my heart. "Now, I have a confession," I say.

Her grin slips. "What is it? Because after that caveman display, I kind of hoped you had more in mind for us back here than talking." She loops her arms around my neck and rubs her breasts against my chest.

I groan at the feel of her nipples digging into my skin beneath the cotton shirt. "We'll get to that. Soon," I promise, dipping my head and running my nose along hers.

Her eyes darken, growing hazy with a desire that matches mine. But it has to wait.

"I have to admit, I kept waiting for you to get bored," I admit. "I thought you'd resent having to work for a living and decide to go back home." I clear my throat. "I knew Preston was an issue, as were your parents' demands. But I didn't want to have my hopes up and my heart broken. Turns out, I underestimated you." I hate to admit I didn't trust her.

"I know."

"What?" How could she have caught onto my feelings? I kept them well-hidden or so I thought.

She laughs for a second, but her expression quickly sobers. "I knew something was bothering you, but I wasn't sure if you thought I was overstaying my welcome, or you were worried about…me leaving." She shrugs. "Based on the things you said when we first met, I knew you didn't trust easily."

"Which things?" I ask warily. I confessed to a few hang-ups about us, but not all.

"Oh, me being too young, our experiences being worlds apart…" She waves a dismissive hand through the air.

"You being a virgin," I go on to add, giving her the rest of what I held back. "And the fact that you'd probably want marriage and kids one day, whereas I swore off both."

The color drains from her face. "You don't want marriage or a family?"

"I didn't." I keep my hand on her jaw, my thumb brushing her soft skin. "Then I met you. Pretty soon I wanted *everything*. But you do have a lot of life to live before we dive into a family."

"And we should still take time to get to learn more and enjoy each other, but I need to know you're in this just like I am," she says, staring into my eyes, her expression hopeful.

My heart squeezes tight in my chest. "If *being in this* means I love you, and I'm not going anywhere, then yeah, I'm in this."

"You love me?" The hesitation in her voice pulls at me and I press my lips over hers, taking my time to show her my feelings without using words.

I'd rather taste her. Her tongue slides against mine, and her fingers thread through my hair, hanging on to me tight. The kiss goes on, and I never want to let her go.

But I force myself to break our connection.

Drawing a deep breath, I inhale the strawberry scent I do not want to live without and meet her gaze. "Yeah, princess. I love you."

Tears fill her eyes. "I love you, too."

"Then why are you crying?" I brush away the moisture on her face.

"Because other than my grandmother and sister, no one's ever said that to me before. And knowing you feel the same way? That's everything."

No, *she* is everything.

"You deserve to be loved. And I'm going to spend every day proving that to you. Because this isn't just a one summer thing. You and me? We're in this for the long term and that includes marriage and kids…"

"And a dog?"

I laugh. "A dog, a cat, a house…anything you want," I say, and then I go about sealing the deal with our mouths and our bodies. Because she is mine. And if I have my way, it will be for a lifetime.

Thanks for reading! What's next?

Remy Sterling and the Sterling Family … with visits by the Kingstons and Dares.
Read JUST ONE MORE MOMENT!

Want even more Carly books?

CARLY'S BOOKLIST by Series – visit:
https://www.carlyphillips.com/CPBooklist

Sign up for Carly's Newsletter:
https://www.carlyphillips.com/CPNewsletter

Join Carly's Corner on Facebook:
https://www.carlyphillips.com/CarlysCorner

Carly on Facebook:
https://www.carlyphillips.com/CPFanpage

Carly on Instagram:
https://www.carlyphillips.com/CPInstagram

Carly's Booklist

newest series listed first

The Dare to Fall Series
Book 1: Falling for Trouble (Rainey & Lucas)
Book 2: Falling for Real (Kaylee & Tristan)
Book 3: Falling for Love (Sophie & Jack)

The Sterling Family
Book 1: Just One More Moment (Remington Sterling & Raven Walsh)
Book 2: Just One More Dare (Dex Kingston & Samantha Dare)
Book 3: Just One More Mistletoe (Max Corbin & Brandy Bloom)
Book 4: Just One More Temptation (Fallon Sterling & Noah Powers)
Book 5: Just One More Affair (Jared Sterling & Charlotte Kendall)
Book 6: Just One More Time (Aiden Sterling & Brooke Snyder)
Book 7: Just One More Date (Leo Watson & Camille Hendricks)

The Dirty Dares
Book 1: Just One Dare (Aurora Kingston & Nick Dare)
Book 2: Just One Kiss (Jade Dare & Knox Sinclair)

Book 3: Just One Taste (Asher Dare &
Nicolette Bettencourt)
Book 4: Just One Fling (Harrison Dare &
Winter Capwell)
Book 5: Just One Tease (Zach Dare &
Hadley Stevens)
Novella: Just One Summer (Maddox James &
Gabriella Davenport)

The Kingston Family
Book 1: Just One Night (Linc Kingston &
Jordan Greene)
Book 2: Just One Scandal (Chloe Kingston &
Beck Daniels)
Book 3: Just One Chance (Xander Kingston &
Sasha Keaton)
Book 4: Just One Spark (Dash Kingston &
Cassidy Forrester)
Just Another Spark – Short Story (Dash &
Cassidy revisited)
Novella: Just One Wish (Axel Forrester &
Tara Stillman)

Dare Nation
Book 1: Dare to Resist (Austin Prescott &
Quinn Stone)
Book 2: Dare to Tempt (Damon Prescott &
Evie Wolfe)
Book 3: Dare to Play (Jaxon Prescott &
Macy Walker)

Book 4: Dare to Stay (Brandon Prescott &
Willow James)
Novella: Dare to Tease (Hudson Northfield &
Brianne Prescott)

** Paul Dare's sperm donor kids*

The Sexy Series
Book 1: More Than Sexy (Jason Dare &
Faith Lancaster)
Book 2: Twice As Sexy (Tanner Grayson &
Scarlett Davis)
Book 3: Better Than Sexy (Landon Bennett &
Vivienne Clark)
Novella: Sexy Love (Shane Warden &
Amber Davis)

The Knight Brothers
Book 1: Take Me Again (Sebastian Knight &
Ashley Easton)
Novella: Take The Bride (Sierra Knight &
Ryder Hammond)
Book 2: Take Me Down (Parker Knight &
Emily Stevens)
Book 3: Dare Me Tonight (Ethan Knight &
Sienna Dare)
Take Me Now – Short Story (Harper Stevens &
Matt Banks)

The New York Dares
Book 1: Dare to Surrender (Gabe Dare &

Isabelle Masters)
Book 2: Dare to Submit (Decklan Dare &
Amanda Collins)
Book 3: Dare to Seduce (Max Savage &
Lucy Dare)

Dare to Love Series
Book 1: Dare to Love (Ian Dare & Riley Taylor)
Book 2: Dare to Desire (Alex Dare &
Madison Evans)
Book 3: Dare to Touch (Dylan Rhodes &
Olivia Dare)
Book 4: Dare to Hold (Scott Dare &
Meg Thompson)
Book 5: Dare to Rock (Avery Dare &
Grey Kingston)
Book 6: Dare to Take (Tyler Dare & Ella Shaw)
A Very Dare Christmas – Short Story (Ian &
Riley revisited)

** Sienna Dare gets together with Ethan Knight in **The Knight Brothers**
(Dare Me Tonight).*
** Jason Dare gets together with Faith in the **Sexy Series** (More Than Sexy).*
** Kaden Barnes (you met him at the end of Dare to Take) has his own book
in **The Billionaire Bad Boys** (Going Down Easy).*

For the most recent Carly books, visit
CARLY'S BOOKLIST page
www.carlyphillips.com/CPBooklist

Billionaire Bad Boys
Book 1: Going Down Easy (Kaden Barnes &
Lexie Parker)
Book 2: Going Down Fast (Lucas Monroe &
Maxie Sullivan)
Book 3: Going Down Hard (Derek West &
Cassie Storms)
Book 4: Going In Deep (Julian Dane &
Kendall Parker)
Going Down Again – Short Story (Kade &
Lexie revisited)

Bodyguard Bad Boys
Book 1: Rock Me (Ben Hollander &
Summer Michelle)
Book 2: Tempt Me (Austin Rhodes &
Mia Atwood)
Novella: His To Protect (Talia Shaw &
Shane Landon)

Serendipity Series
Book 1: Serendipity (Ethan Barron &
Faith Harrington)
Book 2: Kismet (Lissa Gardelli & Trevor Dane)
Book 3: Destiny (Nash Barron & Kelly Moss)
Book 4: Fated (Kate Andrews & Nick Mancini)
Book 5: Karma (Dare Barron &
Liza McKnight)

Serendipity's Finest
Book 1: Perfect Fit (Michael Marsden &
Cara Hartley)
Book 2: Perfect Fling (Erin Marsden &
Cole Sanders)
Book 3: Perfect Together (Sam Marsden &
Nicole Farnsworth)
Book 4: Perfect Strangers (Alexa Collins &
Luke Thompson)

Hot Heroes Series
Book 1: Touch You Now (Halley Ward &
Kane Harmon)
Book 2: Hold You Now (Phoebe Ward &
Jake Nichols)
Book 3: Need You Now (Juliette Collins &
Braden Clark)
Book 4: Want You Now (Andi Harmon &
Kyle Davenport)

The Chandler Brothers
Book 1: The Bachelor (Roman Chandler &
Charlotte Bronson)
Book 2: The Playboy (Rick Chandler &
Kendall Sutton)
Book 3: The Heartbreaker (Chase Chandler &
Sloane Carlisle)

The Lucky Series
Book 1: Lucky Charm (Derek Corwin &
Gabrielle Donovan)
Book 2: Lucky Streak (Mike Corwin & Amber
Rose Brennan)
Book 3: Lucky Break (Jason Corwin &
Lauren Perkins)

Costas Sisters
Book 1: Under the Boardwalk (Ariana Costas &
Quinn Donovan)
Book 2: Summer of Love (Zoe Costas &
Ryan Baldwin)

Ty and Hunter
Book 1: Cross My Heart (Lilly Dumont &
Ty Benson)
Book 2: Sealed with a Kiss (Molly Gifford &
Daniel Hunter)

The Hot Zone
Book 1: Hot Stuff (Annabelle Jordan &
Brandon Vaughn)
Book 2: Hot Number (Micki Jordan &
Damian Fuller)
Book 3: Hot Item (Sophie Jordan & Riley Nash)
Book 4: Hot Property (Amy Stone &
John Roper)

The Simply Series
Book 1: Simply Sinful (Kayla Luck &
Kane McDermott)
Book 2: Simply Scandalous (Catherine Luck &
Logan Montgomery)
Book 3: Simply Sensual (Ben Callahan &
Grace Montgomery)
Book 4: Body Heat (Jake Lowell &
Brianne Nelson)
Book 5: Simply Sexy (Rina Lowell &
Colin Lyons)

The Most Eligible Bachelor Series
Book 1: Kiss Me if You Can (Sam Cooper &
Lexie Davis)
Book 2: Love Me If You Dare (Rafe Mancuso
& Sara Rios)

Carly Classics
Book 1: The Right Choice (Carly Wexler &
Mike Novak)
Book 2: Perfect Partners (Chelsie Russell &
Griffin Stuart)
Book 3: Unexpected Chances (Dylan North &
Holly Evans)
Book 4: Worthy of Love (Kevin Manning &
Nikki Welles)

For the most recent Carly books, visit
CARLY'S BOOKLIST page
www.carlyphillips.com/CPBooklist

Carly's Still Traditionally Published Books

Stand-Alone Books
The Seduction – Kindle Worlds, The
Arrangement Universe – No Longer Available
More Than Words Volume 7 – Compassion
Can't Wait
Naughty Under the Mistletoe
Grey's Anatomy 101 Essay

For the most recent Carly books, visit
CARLY'S BOOKLIST page
www.carlyphillips.com/CPBooklist

About the Author

Carly Phillips is the *NY Times*, *Wall Street Journal*, and *USA Today* bestselling author of over eighty sexy contemporary romances featuring hot men, strong women, and the emotionally compelling stories her readers have come to expect and love. She is happily married to her college sweetheart and lives outside New York City. She is the mother of two adult daughters and a Havanese puppy who stars on her social media and newsletter. Visit her website: www. carlyphillips.com.